Praise for *Beaver Girl*

If beavers spoke and thought human language, they'd probably sound a lot like the clever, soulful protagonists of Cassie Premo Steele's charming novel. *Beaver Girl* is a wonderful contribution to the castor canon that's certain to convert a new wave of Beaver Believers — and a good thing, too, since our semiaquatic brethren need all the supporters they can get!

-Ben Goldfarb, Author of the Bestselling *Eager: The Surprising, Secret Life of Beavers and Why They Matter*

Beaver Girl takes readers into the beautiful landscapes of South Carolina to show us the hope that swims deeply there. This book is the antidote we need in the face of climate change!

-Mary Alice Monroe, *New York Times* Bestselling Novelist

Beaver Girl explores a grim climate future through the eyes of both beavers and people. Although our species differ in many ways, Cassie Premo Steele skillfully illustrates what we have in common - a deep longing for safety, family, and to build a brighter future for the next generation. I was particularly happy to find so many tidbits of actual beaver ecology woven into the story. This is a book that I could easily read for fun or assign in one of the science classes I teach as an example of communicating science through story.

-Emily Fairfax, Assistant Professor of Geography at the University of Minnesota

Both sobering and hopeful, *Beaver Girl* is a story for our times. As Livia flees climate catastrophe, pandemic tragedy and societal collapse, Chap's compassion and wise teachings offer us all another way of living in this troubled world.

-Frances Backhouse, Author of *Once They Were Hats: In Search of the Mighty Beaver and Beavers: Radical Rodents and Ecosystem Engineers*

Beaver Girl is the novel 'beaver believers' have been waiting for. Premo Steele has written an incredibly thoughtful fictionalized account of the relationship between a human and a beaver family that represents beavers' broader positive impacts not only for our degraded yet resilient landscapes, but also for our tender human spirits.

-Alison Zak, director of the Human-Beaver Coexistence Fund and author of *Wild Asana: Animals, Yoga, and Connecting Our Practice to the Natural World*

In Cassie Premo Steele's vivid and endearing novel, *Beaver Girl*, two narrators, human and nonhuman, navigate a changed world with resilience and hope. As they recognize their shared connections with — and responsibilities to — the Earth, they redefine their ideas of family, reminding us that whatever the species, we are all a vital part of our living world.

-Midge Raymond, author of *My Last Continent*

I loved Cassie Premo Steele's *Beaver Girl*. A novel of survival, it is story about seeing beauty amidst devastation and loss. It's about finding a family—human and beyond—into which we can pour our love. And most importantly, *Beaver Girl* offers an invitation to see our world and its many creatures as connected, reliant on each other, so that the world—and all of us—can thrive. There is no better time for this beautiful book.

-Kate Hopper, author of *Ready for Air* and *Use Your Words*

From a near future apocalypse, resonant with contemporary pandemics, catastrophic climate collapse, wildfires, and political unrest, emerges a heartfelt story of human resilience. Livia, a young woman, and Chap, a mature beaver, narrate Cassie Premo Steele's *Beaver Girl*. It is a gripping read that explores survival and care through balance with and connection to the natural world.

-Julie R. Enszer, Editor, *Sinister Wisdom*

Beaver Girl takes readers on a compelling, emotional journey. Cassie Premo Steele shows us that although tragedy finds everyone, love, friendship, and above all, the natural world, will help us heal. This book is essential for our time.

-Amanda K. Jaros, editor of *Labor of Love: A Literary Mama Anthology*

Beaver

Girl

a novel

Cassie Premo Steele

AP / OP

ISBN: 978-1-960882-06-6

Anxiety / Outcast

For Ellis Clare

This novel was written and takes place in the ancestral and unceded territory of the Congaree and Cherokee people, whose cultures revere the wisdom of the beavers as an essential keystone for all life on earth.

Beaver Girl

"[B]eavers can create and maintain wetland habitat that persists through flood, drought, and, as we have shown in this study, fire." -Emily Fairfax and Andrew Whittle, "Smokey the Beaver"

"We need to cure our amnesia, rethink our relationship and acknowledge how much we stand to gain by engaging beavers as keystone partners and climate-change allies." -Frances Backhouse, *Once They Were Hats: In Search of the Mighty Beaver*

"To ecologists, a keystone species is that rare organism that likewise supports an entire biological community...Pull the keystone out, and the arch—or the ecosystem—collapses." -Ben Goldfarb, *Eager: The Surprising Secret Life of Beavers and Why They Matter*

"In most places, a world without beavers is a world without water and the life it supports." -Glynnis Hood, *The Beaver Manifesto*

Livia

I woke to a dream of smoke.

At least, I thought I was dreaming. As the morning light filtered through the gaps in the lavender curtains covering my bedroom window, I realized it was real. The smoke was coming from the east and mixed with the morning sunlight in a sickening yellowish-brown color tinged with a haze of green. It was unlike anything I'd ever seen.

But seeing was not my greatest problem now. The other sense I'd taken for granted – smell – and the ability to breathe without wheezing: these were becoming increasingly more difficult with each second that passed.

My heart pounding as it dawned on me what was happening, I jumped from my bed to stand up, and this only made it worse. My hazel eyes rimmed with red burned as tears fell from them, and my lungs felt as if they'd been ignited.

It was then that I remembered the lesson I'd been taught in elementary school when the firefighters came with their big, shiny red engine to impress the kids and make us pay attention: Stop, drop, and roll.

So I did, crouching down next to my bed and looking around at the floor of the room, which was a tiny bit clearer of smoke, although not clean as it had once been, I realized now as I noticed the dust bunnies underneath the bed and sitting in corners. I'd been alone for a long time now, and somehow dusting had fallen from the regular list of chores that concerned me. Or chores that anyone would tell me to do.

Food. Water. And now fresh air. These were now my greatest concerns.

I saw my green backpack near the door, still filled with a couple of cans of soup I'd managed to scrounge up on my last outing, and my rain jacket that came in handy during the sudden storms that erupted frequently when I was out foraging, along with my Swiss Army knife. I reached up to the table beside my bed and grabbed my water bottle – almost empty – and put it in the bag without taking a sip. I'd learned only to drink when I absolutely could not live with the thirst anymore. I also reached for my journal on the bedside table and placed that carefully into the backpack along with the five pens I had left. These were the only possessions that really meant anything to me now. I opened the drawer underneath and took out a few pairs of socks and underwear and added those. I remembered my mom saying I should always wear clean underwear in case I was in an accident. I guess she meant so I wouldn't be ashamed of first responders or hospital staff seeing my dirty underwear. We were long past that.

After I put on my socks and shoes, I hesitated a moment wondering if I needed to pack more clothes but standing to walk over to my dresser almost took me out as the smoke entered my lungs violently again, and I bolted from the room.

As I left them, I said quick and silent goodbyes to my bedroom where I'd slept for fourteen years since I was five years old, and then to the hallway where my mom had hung dozens of photos of our family, each in its own beautiful frame and balanced perfectly to create a portrait of our life, and then I waved goodbye to the kitchen as I headed for the front door.

Goodbye, sheets. Goodbye, pillow. Goodbye, photos. Goodbye, countertops. Goodbye, cup.

It was like I was reading myself the book, *Goodnight, Moon*, except there was no little old lady in a chair and no rabbit and no hope of waking from the dream in the morning.

And then I braced myself, testing the doorknob to feel how hot it was. The firefighters had taught us to do this, too.

It was warm to the touch, but I covered my hand with the bottom of my t-shirt and turned the knob. As I pulled the door open, I heard a whooshing sound and glass shattering from the kitchen windows.

My leaving coincided with the fire's first entrance into the house. There was a word for this: backdraft? We'd watched a movie about it once, but I pushed away the memory of Friday night family nights with homemade pizzas and movies.

There was no more pizza. No more movies.

Running down my street, energized by the rush of adrenaline from my home being destroyed behind me, I could see that the sun coming up in the east was fully above the horizon now, and as I reached the highest point in the neighborhood, I could see actual flames rising from the land as far as I could see into the eastern distance. Above this was a smoke, darker than the puce that had been hanging in the air only minutes ago when I'd woken in my room. And there were black clouds hovering just above the sun like a heavy and dangerous blanket threatening to smother the light. The firefighters had taught us how to leave our homes safely in a fire but not what to do when the whole world was in flames. And there were no more firefighters, either.

It didn't take me long to decide that east was not the direction I would be taking. I turned to my right, which was west, and, with my lungs beginning to burn again, slowed down to walk for one last time through the neighborhood where I'd lived almost all my life.

Sometimes it comforted me to do the math. As if numbers were bled of emotion and that somehow helped me feel better about the situation.

I moved to this house with my mother when I was five: 14 years ago.

She got remarried when I was six: 13 years ago.

I had my first kiss when I was fifteen: 4 years ago. (I was a nerd, okay?)

I got my driver's license when I was sixteen: 3 years ago.

The virus hit when I was seventeen: 2 years ago.

I last left my house during the day when I was eighteen: 1 year ago.

Well, technically, it had been eight months since I'd left my house during the day. And actually, to be more precise, it had been 232 days. I was counting.

An American flag was ripped and torn but still flying from the porch of one house. It was a few weeks after the Fourth of July, but I suspected the flag had been hung long before that. Curtains on the interior of the windows at the front of the house hung heavy and dark, closed to the sight of the encroaching fires, even though I sensed those curtains had not been opened to any view for quite some time.

Halloween decorations were still on another porch. It was July. I did the math in my head again: 270 days since last Halloween.

There was a neighbor at the corner who used to keep his dog in the side yard, and I remember it would scare me a little when I walked by. My cousin had been bit by a dog when we were toddlers, and the memory of it stayed in my body. The dog was not barking now.

I looked away, and on the other side of the street, blue tarps hung over the roofs on two houses, placed there to keep rain from coming in until they could be fixed. I guessed they'd been there since the time of the last big storm – or maybe one of the storms before that one.

Alongside the house that I considered to be the last in our neighborhood before the larger roads began, there was a little garden patch filled with overgrown collard greens. Our home garden had been a source of these, too, as I discovered that with benign neglect and sufficient rain, they would bear leaves in several seasons.

I picked some leaves now, leaving the roots, of course, for whomever might wander this way in the future, and rolled them up to put in my backpack to eat later. I'd learned that they could be sweet when chewed raw for long enough.

No cars were moving as I headed closer to the nearby four-lane road. Only the sound of one crow cawing from an oak tree – from an expression of loneliness or an attempt to warn others of the fire, I couldn't tell. My mother loved crows. She said you could always tell when some trouble was happening because they'd announce it to the other creatures. Hawk on wing. Squirrel poaching a hidden cache of nuts. Human approaching.

Despite all this evidence of neglect and abandonment, breakdown and breaking apart, though, it struck me that there were still leaves on the trees, and wildflowers were blooming along the edge of the road, pink and lavender, magenta and yellow, and that somehow even though the world as I'd known it had ended, the seasons had turned from winter to spring, and now we were fully into summer.

I had stopped going out during the day that past winter because those few who had survived the triple impact of the virus and the collapse of the world economy and increasing climate disasters had banded together into gangs for protection. And as humans have been known to do, what began as protection escalated into violence against anyone perceived as an outsider.

In other words, I had learned to leave my house only in the dark to avoid more violence.

The electricity grid had failed almost a year before, so streetlights hadn't been an issue. This meant that if I stayed indoors during the day and only went out at night during the times in the month when the moon was dark or the skies were cloudy enough to provide me with adequate cover, I could stay safe.

And all of this made being outside now in the full summer daylight even that much more striking. Nature had gone on without us in all its wild, tangled growth.

I'd forgotten how many colors of green the leaves of trees could be. Emerald, olive, seagrass, jade, lime, olive, khaki, avocado.

"Come on, Livia!" she yelled to me from a rock in the middle of the river. "Don't you dare tell me you're scared!"

"It's so cold," I complained, dipping one foot in the water and smiling at her, knowing I would get there eventually. Mouse had always been more courageous than I was, and faster, and bolder. She'd been my best friend forever, ever since our mothers had met at our preschool. They had told that story over and over – how they met on that first morning while dropping us off, and went out for coffee right after, and eventually became inseparable.

That summer that Mouse and I were seventeen, in addition to the discoveries of freedom that learning how to drive a car had afforded us for the past year, we were also realizing the immense joy that a remote bend in the river could lend.

The green river water was cold and clear as it rushed down and enveloped my body in a soothing relief from the heat of the midday sun. Once I was fully in and had adjusted to the temperature, I swam toward Mouse on the rock and saw her grinning at me. I had always been a strong swimmer.

"Finally!" she exclaimed jokingly as I clambered up the rock. Its surface was smooth and warm, and I spread out to absorb its heat much like several painted turtles were doing on a large rock near the other shore.

I sighed and rolled over to see the bright red and yellow colors on their bodies and then my eyes wandered higher, and I wondered how many trees I could name. Live oak, ash, loblolly pine, tulip poplar: each with their own signature green color, blended all together to make the scenery of what would become later the memory of my last happy day.

Before that summer was even over, the virus would take Mouse away.

That was two years ago.

I tried not to dwell on how lonely I was. It only made things worse.

Most of the time, simply surviving took so much of my mental and physical energy that I could focus on the nighttime tasks at hand – foraging for food, gathering water, hiding from the marauding gangs – that the thoughts of how things used to be could be kept at bay.

But that day, as the fires encroached upon the city from the east and I fled my home for the final time, something about being outside in the daylight and seeing the trees going on in their glorious green summer profusion as if nothing bad could possibly be happening: this confluence of time and flight brought Mouse and all she meant to me back to me.

The dances we choreographed and performed together in third grade and then uploaded to social media before our mothers discovered it and gave us grave lectures about stranger danger.

The middle school dances where we danced with each other and made fun of the boys who were shorter than we were and hadn't yet reached puberty, who sat awkwardly on the bleachers playing games on their phones, too afraid to talk to girls as they lagged at least a year behind us in physical and emotional maturity.

The night in high school when we first tried alcohol, stolen from my mother's liquor cabinet, and swallowed directly from several bottles, and how later we took turns holding each other's hair back as we threw up in the bathroom toilet.

The morning Mouse came into my room when—

That's enough of that, I said to myself, literally shaking my head to shield the memory from my mind.

I stopped walking and took a drink of water from the bottle in my backpack. I'd been moving away from the fires for over an hour and deserved a little sip, I told myself.

The voice of Mouse arose in me again, and I heard her say, "Go to the river."

She was right. I had maybe two ounces of water left in my bottle. And the heat of the fires felt like it was mixing with the rising summer temperature. I certainly did need more water.

"Thanks, Mouse," I said out loud, as I turned left at the next road to head south to the river.

Chap

I woke as I usually did, a short time before sunset in the dark of our lodge, Penny cuddling next to me, and our three little ones on the other side of her.

I listened to their breathing for a while and then it struck me: something was missing from the sounds around me.

I turned my ears forward and back again to gauge if I'd perhaps been mistaken. But no. It was unmistakable.

The silence.

For the first time in my life – which was a longer time than I liked to admit because although I was an older beaver, I was still strong and capable of taking care of my family – there was no birdsong.

I rolled to my side slowly so as not to awake the kits and let my partner get a little more sleep before our nighttime work began, and then I headed down into one of the hallways that connected our lodge above the water to the pond below.

It was a safe entrance that we'd constructed together many years and several litters of kits before. It allowed us to come and go hidden from predators on the land and in the sky, as we could stay underwater for up to fifteen minutes at a time, waiting to listen for sounds and feel for vibrations before venturing out onto the land.

But this evening upon waking, I did not wait the usual amount of time before swimming directly to the bank and scrambling up to balance on my hind legs, tucking my tail beneath me for balance and concentrating hard to watch and listen.

As I looked up into the tallest tree along the bank, an ash filled with light green leaves that rose over two hundred feet from the forest floor into the air, I scanned the branches for the movement of wings.

Nothing.

I let my eyes peer into the deep green needles of loblolly pine trees where nuthatches and woodpeckers lived.

Silence.

I tilted my head toward the most generous of trees in the swamp: the cypress who was able to live in the water like us because its roots rose from the liquid like human knees in order to be able to take in enough air.

Stillness.

I felt my heart beating underneath the soft inner fur of my chest, and my breath caught. What could be happening to make the birds disappear? Usually at this time of day as the sun tilted down toward the opposite side of the river, the forest was a raucous chorus as all the birds began their thanksgiving song for the day.

All my life, I had been waking to the sound of this symphony, a lullaby in reverse, cheering me and providing me with energy for all the cutting and grinding and slicing and hauling I would do all night long.

But not tonight.

Tonight, I decided as the sun slipped lower, I needed to forego my usual labor and go outside our territory in the swamp to see what was happening.

"Chap?" my partner purred quietly next to me on the bank. So she was awake. "What's happening?" she asked.

"I don't know, Penny," I admitted to her. "But I'm going to try to find out."

She nodded, rubbing her front paws together on top of her belly as she balanced on her hind legs like me. She often did this when she was anxious.

I knew she was anxious now. So was I. But I also knew she trusted me. We'd been together almost all our lives – since our third years when we first found each other on a large rock formation along the riverside one spring morning about a year after leaving our parents' lodges.

"Be careful, Chap," she murmured to me softly.

"I will, Penny," I promised. "Will you be alright with the little ones on your own for a while?" I asked her.

I knew the answer. In the same way that she trusted me to venture off and try to discover what had happened to the birds, I knew that I could rely upon her to guard our kits on her own. We'd been together so long that we knew each other completely in this way. But I wanted to ask her anyway. It was only polite.

"Of course," she chittered, her back teeth rubbing along the long front ones to sharpen them. I knew that meant she was preparing to head to the cypress tree she'd been working on the night before.

I poked my nose against the side of her face and nuzzled her, inhaling her unique castoreum scent of berries and vanilla as it rose from her body and gave me strength for my uncertain journey ahead.

"Be careful," she whispered. "I love you."

"I love you," I replied, and headed away from our pond and into the forest.

I moved so much more slowly over land than I could swim in the water that it was frustrating. Additionally, I needed to stop often to sniff and listen for predators because my slow movement made me so much more vulnerable on land.

I'd gone about three and a half miles when I spotted it in the air: smoke.

I propped my tail a little closer to my rear to be able to stand a bit taller, and I breathed in deeply several times, letting the scent roll around in my nose and enter my brain.

It was coming from the direction where morning comes. Morning usually means an end to work for the night and the respite of returning to the lodge with a full belly and a growing cache of additional food stored away.

But not tonight.

I scrambled up atop a large rock that jutted from the forest floor to gain more height and smelled again.

Many trees had already died in the fire. I could smell the smoke of their charred bodies in the air. I nodded my head in silent reverence to them.

Animals, too, had been taken: just from the limited perspective of my perch alone, I could smell foxes, bobcats, and a few wild hogs.

This was why the birds were silent. They'd headed west to the river in hopes that the water there would save them should the fires encroach even closer.

The waxing moon was nowhere to be seen, already descended into the west, which meant the night was halfway over, and the ground would begin to fill up with dew soon, making the sound of approaching predators more muffled.

I recalled my partner's voice telling me to be careful. So, I decided that I'd been away from our territory long enough, and I turned around to head back home in the dark.

White fire greeted me.

Two piercing points glowing between the black shadows of the bodies of trees.

Every hair on my body stood up in alert attention.

24

Had he seen me?

Without a sound, I slouched down as quickly as I could, moving my round body against the smoothness of the large, flat rock formation where I'd been standing only a moment before.

Would the smell of smoke in the air camouflage my smell? I hoped against hope that it would, but even as I lay like a snake against the hard stone, I could smell his harsh ammonia scent: coyote.

And I knew that if I could smell him, the chances were great that he could also smell me, too.

I moved my front right paw as silently as I could around me on the rocks, searching for an opening in which to hide.

Nothing.

Then I stretched out my front left paw.

I found a crack!

Could it be enough for my body to slip into and escape?

I had no choice. I had to take a chance. I dove into the crack between the large rocks and squished myself as small as I could.

The sound of my movement attracted the coyote's attention. The vibrations in the rock against my body as his muscular legs walked across the rock to come closer to me were terrifyingly strong.

I held my breath. I tried to will my heartbeat to quiet down. I thought about Penny and our kits. I waited.

The coyote scraped one of his paws into the crevice that hid me, and somehow, I managed to make myself even smaller.

The paw swiped. Once. Twice. Grazed my fur but missed my flesh both times. He lifted his paw to try again.

And then there was a dreadful cracking sound.

The coyote swung his paw back to wheel around on all fours and face in that direction. Both of us, prey and predator, were frozen and united in our horror as we heard the fire encroaching for the first time into the beloved forest that was our home. We were immobilized together as we witnessed the fire take its first victim: a tulip poplar tree over a century old.

As the flames rose in the tree's huge canopy, the bright orange sight sent the coyote running, probably to give the news to the rest of his pack.

And as soon as he was gone and I felt the coast was clear, I ran, too, as fast as I could, wishing once again that I could be as swift on land as I could be in water. I did not stop until I plopped with a sigh of relief into our pond.

But the relief did not last long.

Livia

The southern city named after Christopher Columbus where I had grown up had been built by European colonists hundreds of years before near a confluence of three rivers. And I had learned from my mother and Katrina, if not my teachers, that this was also where the native people called the Congaree were living when the whites first arrived.

I thought about this, the beginnings and endings of civilizations and how what we used to call civilized was not always so, as I was heading toward the Congaree River that ran straight through the downtown area of the city.

This was not a risk I would usually take, but the heat was rising, and the fires were coming closer, and my need for water was so great. I moved deliberately and slowly, though, not just because of the summer humidity and the thickening smoke in the air, but because I wanted to avoid contact with other humans at all costs.

It had cost me too much before.

I crouched beneath bushes that had once been landscape accents and were now overgrown and literally bushy, walking in a half crawl behind them. I paused behind the larger tree trunks that lined the city streets, using them as cover, running from one to the other as I'd seen people do in war movies. When I could, I took advantage of culverts and alleyways, making sure to watch for movement in them before proceeding into these smaller spaces with fewer chances for escape.

In this way, I traversed the four miles to the river in three hours.

I couldn't know, of course, what other cities looked like in the aftermath of the civilization's collapse, but in my city, the vines and trees and greenery had reclaimed their territory.

Kudzu covered some of the smaller buildings along the downtown streets, swallowing them whole and making them look like the life-sized green dinosaurs I'd seen in a museum in New York City. Ivy ran up the taller buildings, covering the windows like a set in some British murder mystery show where the gardener had been the first one to go. Small weeds that had previously been controlled by pesticides were now tall wildflowers, and grasses rose from the cracks in the sidewalks and streets and waved to me in the hot breeze as I passed by.

The breeze also carried the stench of collapse. I remembered the moment I'd first heard the phrase, "climate collapse." They'd been talking about "climate change" since before I was born, but then there was a sudden turn. And this became fodder for arguments between politicians and corporations and the whole thing struck me as ridiculous because this euphemism couldn't possibly bear the weight of what was actually occurring.

Death. Decay. Mortality. Murder. Loss. Leaving. Rot. Putrid decomposition. That was exactly what I was smelling as I walked the abandoned streets of the city, my footsteps echoing the only sound I was hearing.

Because it was quiet. No traffic. No airplanes. No trains or busses. Of course, it had been this way for months, and I'd gotten used to it at home, but it was quite striking to witness it in the middle of downtown. I thought of the ghost towns in the old westerns, where sagebrush formed big, dry circular formations that swept through the abandoned dirt roads and crumbling wooden buildings.

Except this was no movie. And this was no longer a town. I was walking now through a ghost world.

And I was glad of it. Because it meant I was encountering no people in it.

By the time I could see the riverbank, it was the middle of the afternoon, and my thirst was so terrible that my tongue felt like an alien beast, a dry and prickly reptile with sharp claws and long teeth, that had colonized my mouth.

All I could think about was water. I could hear the river rapids running over the smooth rocks. I wanted to become stone. I wanted the cool liquid within me and without lest my body become a desiccated fossil, a reminder of what I used to be.

That was when I made my mistake.

So eager was I to reach the river that I started to walk, out in the open, the last fifty yards.

This was something that I would go over repeatedly in my mind, later - what I could have done differently.

I could have waited and watched for movement first.

I could have ducked beneath the bridge and scooted in the shadows to the water's edge.

I could have kept going to a part of the river not accessed by road or bridge, where it would be less likely that I would encounter people.

People.

That word used to mean something. In my parched and colonized mouth now, it had the bitter taste of metal and blood.

"Hey, pretty, where are you going?" the voice said.

It was male. And had that mock humorous tone that portended no good. The kind that would take offense if you didn't speak back in a similarly jovial way. We'd seen politicians and public figures adopt this attitude over the years, and it had spread like a virus to the general population.

I froze. The river was only a few yards away, and I could hear the water rushing over the rocks in the center and lapping against the muddy shore nearby. The reptile in my mouth clawed against my tongue instinctively.

"To the river," I said, my lips cracking against the sound of my voice, out loud. I pointed with my arm to show him where I meant to go.

"For a swim?" he asked and smiled, and as he did, I could see within the scraggly brown beard that surrounded his face and between his parched lips that his teeth were rotted. Black. Stumps. The hair on his head hung down long and greasy.

"Want company?" he asked, still smiling.

I froze. I knew from past experience that to say no too soon could trigger further aggression.

"Not a swim," I said, trying to smile back at him, taking my water bottle out of my backpack to show him. There was literally one drop left in it, and my dry tongue curled in anticipation of more.

"I need water," I said. "To drink."

"Well, you won't be getting any," he said, shaking his head slowly and making a sad face.

I was not sure what he meant. I wasn't sure if he meant to stop me from accessing the riverbank or if there was something else happening. I detected a hint of actual sorrow in his voice.

"Why not?" I asked.

"Sewage pipe burst upstream," he said, pointing north. "Let out tons of crap. Literally."

I thought of the foul stench that hit my nostrils as I approached the center of the city. I could feel my heart beating beneath my chest. The fact that the water would be polluted had never occurred to me.

At first, the virus overloaded the medical system and people's health began to suffer from not getting regular health care, and then the numbers of sick and dead or simply quarantined meant the supply chains were slowing. And this caused panic.

For some reason I still didn't quite understand, the next domino to fall, literally, was that the cell phone towers were destroyed by rival gangs, as people turned against each other and tried to cut off access to communication to gain the upper hand. Of course, this in turn made things worse for everybody.

Then the power grid had rolling blackouts, as earthquakes cascaded from the coastal regions to the interior of the continent and disrupted the ability of power companies to keep their supply routes going on land and online. And then it failed completely.

This meant that there had been no fuel for transportation or heating for almost a year now. It had been a long winter.

And now it was summer, and fire was approaching the city.

All this had happened, one catastrophe after another, but for some insane reason, because the city was so close to rivers and my neighborhood was filled with lakes and ponds, I always thought there would be water. Clean water. Accessible water. Drinkable water.

"I could help you, though," he said, softly, walking slowly toward me the way you'd approach a wounded animal. "Maybe we could work out a deal?"

He'd gotten close enough that I could smell him – sourness and terror rose from him like smoke from the fires behind us.

He was afraid, too. Was that possible?

I took a chance.

"What kind of deal?" I asked.

"My friend scored some water purifying tablets from the REI store months ago before it got completely cleaned out. He's forward thinking like that. And we are offering them to people - a select group of people, mind you. Not just anyone. You can't trust just anyone anymore."

I nodded, trying to show him I appreciated his used car salesman approach lest it turn into something more ominous. Scarcity conditions and the effects of unequal access almost always did.

"We could make a trade," he said, lifting his eyebrows as if this idea had just occurred to him.

I narrowed my eyes. "What kind of trade?"

"What do you have in that backpack?" he said, gesturing and taking a step closer to me. His eyes were bloodshot, his skin was yellowish and sweaty, and his breath smelled like what he'd told me had drained into the river to pollute the water itself.

I made a quick mental inventory: a couple cans of soup, my rain jacket, underwear, and socks, and my journal and pens – none of those things would be valuable to him – but my Swiss Army knife. He would want that.

But could I survive without it?

Could I survive without water, though?

There had to be another option.

I took the backpack off my back and held it in front of me like a shield. He was close enough that he could touch me if he wanted.

"How do I know you really have the water tablets?" I asked. "Can I see them?"

He smiled without parting his lips. The pupils of his eyes expanded.

"Don't trust me, eh?" he said.

"Don't trust anybody," I answered, my voice completely flat.

"Smart girl," he said, gesturing behind him. "They're in our van, over there. It broke down months ago, and there's no gas anyway, but it makes a good shelter. I stay there with my friend. The one who pilfered the filters." He laughed, amused at his rhyme. I wondered briefly what he'd done before all this. Who had he been? We were all different now.

"If you follow me, I can show you," he said. "And we can conduct our trade in the privacy of the van."

I still hadn't told him what was in my backpack. And it was clear now that he didn't mean to make a trade of goods. What he was after was a service.

I shifted my backpack away from my body, turning slightly away from him as I hoisted it up and inserted my arms back into the straps.

"Sure," I nodded. "Lead the way."

And as he turned to head toward the van, I bolted in the opposite direction. No longer did I take precautions, watching for humans, taking the hidden routes behind trees and bushes along the way. There was no time for that. I had a life to save.

The backpack thumped against my back as I ran, taking a street that headed slightly downhill so I could gain as much speed as possible.

"Hey!" I heard him yell, and my next breath came a bit easier as I heard the distance between his voice and my body.

I kept going. Footsteps approaching.

I saw a woman hovering in a doorway, leaning sideways, barely conscious, holding out her hand as if I would stop to give her something. They used to call this panhandling. But there was no fuel to cook in pans anymore, and no one was handling anything very well.

I increased my speed, turned left at the next street, and ran until my lungs burned so much from the smoke and lack of water that I had to stop.

Between my heavy breaths as I bent over, my hands on my knees to recover, I heard a woman's voice shriek a sharp, "No!"

She had reached out her hand to ask me for something. But she was the one who ended up giving something to me.

I began to walk as quickly as I could without making any noise. If I could hear them, they could hear me.

He had found someone for his deal.

And this time, it hadn't been me.

Chap

After I returned to our lodge, as the sun rose outside and our three yearlings slept soundly, I huddled as far away from them as I could to tell Penny what I had seen.

"It's getting worse," I said.

"Worse? How?" she asked.

"There's fire. It's coming from the direction where the sun rises but it's headed in our direction."

"How fast?" she asked. "How long do we have?"

"I don't know," I answered honestly. I was an expert with water, but fire was a whole other element entirely, and I did not know its ways. I did know that it would keep moving, though, without something to block it. That was the nature of all things- to move.

This was something I had learned from living in the water way.

In my mind, I pictured our territory. We had constructed six dams around us, and our pond connected to other beds of water through watery routes we'd dug together over the years with our litters. The river was not too far away, but it was in the opposite direction of the fire, so that wouldn't be a sufficient brake until after it had traversed our territory.

"Should we flee?" Penny asked quietly.

I knew what a great risk that would be, and she did, too.

It had taken us a long time to find this area in which to build and be safe for ourselves and our litters. Fleeing would mean starting over again, searching for uninhabited land with access to water, putting ourselves at risk of contact with predators on land, and even contending with other beaver families who would be as equally aggressive about defending their lodges as we were.

I shook my head and rubbed one paw across my face.

"I don't think so, Penny," I said finally. "I think it's best to stay."

I knew that one day I might come to regret my decision if anything should happen to Penny and the kits.

But I wasn't ready to abandon all the work we'd put into making our waterland so safe and secure.

"Oh, Chap," Penny sighed, shaking her head and ringing her paws as she did when she was anxious.

"I know, I know," I murmured to her and nudged the side of my body against her.

"It'll be okay," I promised.

But I didn't even know if I believed myself.

I tried to settle into sleep, but in the middle of that day, earlier than I usually wake to start work, I heard something startling.

I could tell from the vibrations that extended even into the lodge in the middle of the watery pond that it was not bird or animal that I was hearing: these steps were bipedal.

And I smelled them. It was a smell of hunger and fear and desperation. I'd smelled it before when Penny and I were first searching for land to create our home and we'd come across a beaver who'd been caught in a trap.

Beavers sometimes would bite off their own foot to escape.

This species, though, would turn their cruel intentions upon others when despair set in.

Humans.

"This looks good," I heard one say. Male.

"Let's test it first," said the other. Also male.

I felt and heard the ripples in the pond as they submerged an object. It was silent. I longed to leave the lodge to watch them, but I didn't dare.

"Yep," the second one spoke again. "Clean."

"Hallelujah," said the first one, and then I heard sloshing and gurgling as they drank the water and filled containers with it.

"This is such a relief," one of them said. "I was so thirsty!"

I was no longer tracking which one was speaking because what I heard next filled me with terror.

"We'll have to remember this spot in the future."

When I was a yearling in my parents' lodge, I had heard a bomb go off that destroyed a dam nearby, and this sentence reverberated within me just as that sound had done. I wanted to cry out with a yelp or smash my tail into the water in alarm, but I took a deep breath and let it out as slowly as I could so I didn't wake my family or call attention to our lodge.

I couldn't sleep the rest of the day.

I lay in the dark shadows of our lodge as the sun headed west and the smoke grew more intense, listening to the soft snoring of my mate and kits, worrying about them and what would become of us.

Maybe I had been wrong. Maybe we did need to leave and try to find a new waterland, as Penny had suggested.

It had been a warm and foggy late spring morning when I'd left the lodge where my parents had raised me for the first two years of my life. I told myself that the pond I knew as my home, my playground, my food source, and training station was somehow seeping into the air all around me to provide me with the security and sustenance I'd need all on my own.

"Chap," my father said to me as we sat on the steep bank above the eastern shore. "You are ready. You have learned your lessons well, and you can do this. I believe in you."

I wanted to cry but I didn't let myself. Not until my mother joined us.

Waddling up and turning back to face the water so she still could keep an eye on the young ones paddling around in the water, she lifted her head to show me her neck – an invitation to take my last cuddle there.

I bowed my head and let the soft fur beneath her chin swaddle me as she said all she could not say. I felt the messages in touch: she loved me and was proud of me and would remember me always.

I did cry then. And I was not ashamed.

Tears, too, are part of the water way.

I sensed the younger beavers in the water grow still as they watched their oldest brother crying.

And then it was time to go.

I made my way to the creek that flowed into the southeastern side of our pond, dove in, and I was gone.

Of course, I'd been on my own before. My mother and father had given me chores that tested my ability to avoid predators and travel safely and process pieces of trees for our lodge and cache. But always before I knew in my mind that I would return to them after my work was done. Not this time.

This time, there would be no returning and I was on my own to create a home.

The motion of leaving: this, I knew, was also one of the principles of the water way.

Finally, I felt the slight dip in temperature as the sun began her descent behind the river, and I heard the kits stirring and waking Penny with their soft squeals and grunts of sunset happiness. They knew darkness meant it was time to eat and work, and they showed the same joy at the prospect of these activities that Penny and I always had.

The memory of my leaving the lodge of my parents made wider ripples in my mind and receded, and I found myself returning fully to the present and the starting point where our kits were gathered: this place. This was our home. We would stay.

Respecting the source and origin, too, is the code of the water way.

I shook my head to try to erase the knowledge of the human voices that I'd heard and prepared myself to be the protector of this family once again.

"Papa," the littlest kit whispered to me – we'd taught them always to be quiet, even in the lodge. "I was thinking I might try my teeth on the small cedar tonight if you think I'm up to it."

I smoothed her silky back with my paw, which had the effect of soothing my worries, as well, and said, "Yes, of course, Gigi. You're ready."

The cedar was one of the harder trees to harvest, and a kit had to have developed the strength in jaw and teeth to tackle it. But with the changes I'd witnessed the night before, I feared that this, my littlest one, would have to have greater strength than she knew at the time, and I was happy to give her a challenge to test it.

Gigi smiled, "Thanks, Papa," she said. "Can we go now?"

She was eager and it made me proud.

I looked over at Penny.

"Okay," I said. "But come quietly. Let's let your ma sleep a little longer. She was up later than usual to greet me when I returned."

We padded softly to the entrance of the lodge at the bottom of the main hallway, and I dove silently into the pond. As soon as my body entered the water, I felt lighter, both physically and emotionally. I swam the perimeter of the pond to make sure it was safe, and then I signaled to Gigi that she could join me in the water.

As she circled around me, I blew soft bubbles and stretched, feeling my fur and muscles, blubber and skin, all my mind and body, relaxing and finding their center.

I had made the right decision after all, I decided. We would stay. This was our home. This was our water. This was the place that would shelter us, come what may.

Livia

As soon as I'd run far enough that I was sure he wasn't following me anymore, my eyes were drawn to the skies. Hundreds of birds were careening over the city from east to west, heading away from the fire and back toward the river. I knew I'd have to return there, too. Nature had always known more than humans, and we'd been sorely mistaken when we'd ignored the signs before.

I drew a deep breath, felt it reverberate with flutters of resilience in my belly, and kept going.

Dusk descended as I neared the water again, this time away from the downtown area and farther south. I walked slowly, stopping to hide and listen before moving closer to the shore. I hadn't quite figured out what I was going to do about the contamination in the river – or if that had even been a true story – but I did know that the fire was heading this way and being in the water may be my only chance to survive.

When I reached the edge, I bent down and put my hands in. I made a cup of them and brought water to my nose to sniff. I couldn't tell if it was safe to drink or not. It simply smelled like river to me. Like summer and warm rocks and painted turtles and Mouse.

And then I saw it.

Resting atop a large, flat rock like the ones Mouse and I had spent long afternoon hours lounging on during that summer we were seventeen – a red kayak. And what looked like it could be the tip of a black paddle sticking up in it, too.

I couldn't believe it.

Was I hallucinating? I hadn't had water for hours and I hadn't eaten all day, and I'd walked over ten miles at least.

I looked around to see if an owner for the kayak might be nearby. No sound except the soft tapping of the waves on the shore where I was standing. And some birds in the west across the river calling out to mark the sun's going down in the sky.

I sat back onto a dry patch on the riverbank and took off my shoes and socks and put them into my backpack, then rolled up my pants and stood back up again.

This wasn't the first time I'd stolen something – almost all my food had been pilfered from abandoned stores and homes in the past year – but I'd never attempted something this big. Bigger still, though, than the old admonition in me against stealing was my desire to flee. To get away from this city and what remained of the people in it.

My birthday was in July, and I turned sixteen the summer before the virus came. Mouse was a few months younger, so I'd been the first of us to get a license to drive.

"Can we go?" I asked my mom one warm and muggy summer afternoon. "With the car?"

She knew we'd been hanging out at the river on our days off from the ice cream shop where we had summer jobs, but she'd always been the one to drop us off and pick us up again. This would be the first time we went on our own.

I saw her eyes dart to Katrina, who shrugged her shoulders slightly and grinned. "It's up to you, Isabelle," she said gently.

As much as they'd shared mothering us since we were in kindergarten, in times like these, they deferred to each other when it came to making decisions for each daughter they'd brought to the family.

My mom took a deep breath in and held it. Finally, she exhaled and said, "You know what to do."

I nodded.

"Be careful," she said.

I nodded again, and grinned, walked over to her where she was sitting on the couch and placed my chin on the top of her head where her long, soft brown hair began.

"Don't worry, Mamabelle," I said, using the nickname I'd given her back when I was little and learned the name other people called her.

I took the car keys from the ceramic bowl on the exact spot on the kitchen counter where they always were, and Mouse and I headed to the front door.

I didn't take the highway, but on the first four-lane road that went by strip malls and fast-food restaurants, I allowed myself to go faster than I ever had before.

Mouse turned off the air conditioning, and we opened all the windows in the car. The air was humid and heavy, almost filled with water as it always was on late summer afternoons in our city, but it wasn't foggy, and it wasn't raining.

It was just a beautiful, sunny summer day, and Mouse and I felt freedom in the humid wind.

I felt another kind of freedom now, on another late summer day, but this time it came from the water itself that embraced me in its cold but comforting touch as I waded slowly, bending to hold onto one rock after another to keep my balance, my toes dipping into the soft silt at the bottom of the river. And then I was there.

I pulled the kayak as quietly as I could from the rock, aware that the scraping sound could alert others to my presence, and then stepped in and took a seat. It rocked slightly in the motion of the water, and for a moment, I relaxed like a baby in a cradle.

This made me smile.

Because it was my birthday. And maybe this kayak was a birthday present. And maybe I could be a baby just for an instant, and the water of the river could allow me to begin again.

But beginning again takes work. So I got to work. I pulled off my backpack and strapped it into the bungee cords at the back of the boat, picked up the paddle, and started to row south. Downstream. Mostly letting the current take me. Allowing nature to help me, I smiled once again and then breathed a sigh of relief for the first time all day.

The sun went down in the west on my right, but I could still see the glow from the fires in the east to my left.

Once I passed under the last bridge near the city, the river widened and flattened and the current calmed. My mind and heart were calmer, too, but I could hear the complaints coming from my belly: I was terribly hungry. I took advantage of the flowing current and put the paddle down, turned to get my backpack, and used one of the tools on my Swiss Army knife to open my second-to-last can of food: a lentil soup.

"It's best with balsamic vinegar on it," Mouse's mother said to me as she handed me a piping hot bowl of homemade lentil soup. "That's how my Oma served it."

Mouse's grandmother had been German and had married a black American stationed near her hometown, and to hear Katrina tell it, there was no better woman who ever lived. Oma knew about herbs for medicine, she baked her own breads every morning, and she made the world's best soups. Even after Katrina moved to the United States, she stayed close to her parents who'd remained in Germany through frequent phone calls and yearly visits.

Katrina had cooked one of Oma's soups for Mouse and me for lunch one Sunday when we were in elementary school.

I shook a bit of the balsamic vinegar from the bottle on the table into my soup bowl and dipped my spoon into the soup, tasted it, then looked up and smiled.

"The best, right?" said Katrina, and I nodded my head. It really was.

The memory sustained me as much as the calories in the can of cold soup did, and I felt my hands stop shaking and my heart rate slowing and my belly relaxing as my whole body responded to the first nourishment of the day.

"Happy birthday," I whispered quietly to myself before tucking the can back into my backpack and picking up the paddle again.

I was far from the city now, could not see any high-rise buildings in the distance anymore, nor any glows from the fires, and the smoke seemed to have somewhat dissipated out here over the water, as well.

Should I stop and get some sleep, I wondered. It had been a long and harrowing day. Who knew what lay ahead for me when the sun rose again?

"What would Oma do?" I heard Mouse say to me in my mind. I could almost see her in the dark in the boat next to me. Her brown eyes were so kind. They were how she'd gotten her name – her grandfather said she had the dark eyes of a mouse, and she decided she liked this better than the name Martha that she'd been given.

"Oma would keep going," I said to the imaginary Mouse next to me, and then I picked up the paddle again and began to row.

"Mom, why is Mouse's mom your best friend?"

It was bedtime, and I was four years old. We'd known Mouse and her mom, Katrina, for two years. When I was little, I often used this quiet time after my mom read a story to me to ask some kind of deeply existential question. I was a weird kid.

"What an odd question, Livia!" my mom said. "Why do you ask?"

The truth was I knew why I was best friends with Mouse: she was courageous and smart and funny, and we laughed together all the time. But I sensed something else was going on underneath my mom's friendship with Katrina, and I didn't know how to talk to her about it.

"I don't know," I said, backing down.

My mom looked out the window of my bedroom and was quiet for a while.

"She's so kind to me," she said finally. In a soft voice.

I nodded. I knew it. I opened my arms to give my mom a hug. My father hadn't been very kind to her. I knew that. I had pictures in my head of that.

"I love you, Mom," I said.

"I love you, too, baby girl," she said and kissed me on my forehead. "Night night."

I paused in my rowing and looked up at the stars above the river. I'd gone far enough now that I couldn't smell the smoke anymore, and the stars seemed to be winking at me as I remembered my conversation with my mom from when I was four.

Was my mother up there? Was Mouse? And Katrina? Or Oma? Did the dead become stars watching over us or something else? I didn't know. There were so many dead now. It seemed the sky should be more crowded. When the new virus began to ravage the world, there was no time for grieving. And even gathering to do so would have tempted the virus to jump even faster.

So there had been no funeral for Mouse that summer. Or for her Oma still in Germany. Or Mouse's mother within weeks of that. Or for my mother the year after.

I was the only one in our family who had survived. All I had were my backpack, my water bottle, my jacket, my knife, my journal and pens, a few pairs of socks and underwear, and one more can of lentil soup. And this kayak. And a paddle.

But I was a survivor.

Chap

As the sunlight stopped, our work began in earnest.

Penny worked on a tulip poplar from the night before, using her bottom teeth to shave away the sweet pieces just below the bark, sometimes stopping to chew and swallow, other times leaving them in a pile to feed to the young ones later.

As I'd promised she could do, Gigi began working on her own small cedar nearby- close enough that we could keep an eye out for her, but not so close that Penny's tulip poplar or my longleaf pine would fall on her when they eventually toppled.

The two boys harvested sticks from the large trunks of trees that we'd felled previously along the bank – bending their heads at an angle and chewing close to the intersections between branches and thick bark. Their job was to take these still green pieces back to the lodge, but in all honesty, they spent more time chasing and wrestling in the water than they did getting any work done.

It was okay. Play was part of the water way of learning and growing, too.

I hadn't had time to talk to Penny about the humans I'd heard talking and gathering water from our pond earlier in the day while she'd been sleeping. Part of me wondered if it would be wiser just to keep this information to myself so I didn't worry her further. But I also knew a deeper truth. Knowledge is like water, and that everything is connected, and the health of one part depends on the health of the whole. I would tell her as soon as I had a chance, I decided.

Pines are soft, and I was simply shaving pieces of it for bedding, so my tree was relatively easy work, and it gave me time to think and remember.

My own father had been very old when I was born, and I'd been the only male in his last litter with my mother. But this also meant he had years and years of wisdom to pass on to me, his last son.

I'd learned about the ways of water from him.

"The humans think water is soft," he told me. "And they use it as a plaything, much like young kits do. But it's the opposite of soft."

"What do you mean?" I'd asked, taking my mouth briefly away from a lily pad leaf I'd rolled up and held between my small front paws to chew on. "Water is hard? I don't understand."

"It's hard as in strong," he said. "Floods can destroy whole forests. Even the humans are afraid of floods. And the work we do helps prevent that from happening. As we create dams to distribute the water into shallow ponds and foraging creeks, we teach the water which way to go so it doesn't overwhelm an area. We can teach it this balance because we respect its strength."

I nodded, chewing on the sweet green lily leaf.

"But water can also be hard in another sense," he continued. "Humans know this increasingly more day by day. A lack of water can destroy life in even more brutal ways than floods."

My round brown eyes grew wide. "Drought?" I whispered.

"Yes," he said.

I'd heard the word but never said it myself. It scared me even to hear it out loud.

"We also allow the water to hide underground so that during the times when the rains don't come, there can be enough in storage."

I knew what he meant. He'd shown me places in the forest where his ancestors had built ponds, and now they were green meadows fed by underground reservoirs.

But then a thought occurred to me, and it scared me even more than the idea of drought.

If his ancestors had built ponds that were no longer there, did that mean that this pond, our home, would one day also be gone? And that my father, too, would someday disappear?

I swallowed the piece of sweet lily pad I'd been chewing, and it lay like an unchewed wood chip in my throat.
Even though I didn't say anything, my father sensed I was anxious.

"Enough water lessons for today," he smiled. "How would you like to check on the farthest dam with me right now?"

This was a privilege that only kits in training to leave their parents' lodge were given. It was fairly safe going because my family had built canals that we could travel in from one watery area to another. But there was still great risk since we would be so far from our lodge.

"Of course!" I replied. "I'd love to go!"

I looked over at my kits, only a year old. It would be another year before they left our lodge, so that meant they were not yet the age I'd been when my father took me on that journey. It also meant that it was up to Penny and me to provide for them for another year, and despite all the hard work we did night after night, the signs were there that the world was not as safe as it had been when I was younger.

I heard the familiar cracking of wood, a bit like thunder in the night, and it meant that the lightning strike of timber falling would follow.

We'd taught the kits to dive for cover when they heard it, and I saw that they did, tearing away from the work they'd been doing and diving swiftly into the water to swim away. Soon after I joined them, and Penny did, too. From deep beneath the surface of the water, we heard the humming of the paw-like leaves of the tulip poplar tree moving through the night air as the tree fell, and then we felt the reverberations within the land beneath us and the water around us as the hardwood tumbled to the ground. A life of growing for that tree had come to an end.

But it was not at the end completely, for the fallen tree only heralded the true beginning of our time with it, as all of us would work on processing the leaves and twigs, branches, bark, and trunk. Some we would eat in the nights to come – especially that sweet part called cambium just underneath the surface. Other portions would go into reinforcing the dams around us or plugging holes in the bottom of ponds. Small scraps would be brought into the lodge for fresh bedding, giving a sweet, lemony smell to our home. Everything would be useful. Nothing would be wasted.

It was my father who'd taught all this to me. As I floated on my back calmly in the pond with my family around me, I was grateful that the smoke I'd smelled earlier in the day seemed to have dissipated, and I was able to look up to a clear night sky filled with stars.

The stars were our lights and companions, I'd learned as a young kit. They helped us in our endeavors even when the moon did not show up for work. I remembered how I saw them blinking when I was young, and I felt somehow that they were cheering us on, even when the cutting and hauling was exhausting.

I felt this way now, too – cheered and resolute.

Piece by piece, my family would work with me to honor the great and long life of that decades-old tulip poplar tree, and in this way, the trees and the water, the land and the stars, thrived together with our help.

Penny was already directing our two yearlings, Henry and Mack, to bundle up the leaves to take to our cache, and Gigi had returned to her small cedar tree to gather up as many chips as she could in her front paws.

I took one more moment to look up at the stars and thank them for their light, and they glimmered back at me.

Livia

I traveled down the river through the night, fortified by the lentil soup in my belly, the sparkling stars overhead me, and the air, cooler and clearer than it had been in the city. As the first wash of lavender light flowed up in the east, I felt my fatigue and knew I had to stop and see where my nighttime river journey had taken me.

I also knew I needed to hide.

Traveling in the daylight, alone, as a woman, in a bright red kayak out on the water- this was not the wisest survival move.

Unfortunately, the western side of the river was steep and rocky, and I could see no place to bring the kayak onto the land safely, either for it or for me, so I rowed the kayak to the eastern bank where there was a soft, sandy shore between the water and the trees.

Even the bottom of the boat seemed to sigh as it rested there, and I felt gravity and exhaustion weigh down on me, too. I pulled the boat a bit more into the forest, found a few downed branches still holding onto their brown leaves to cover it as best I could, and then looked around.

No path. That was good. It meant I'd reached an area that was hopefully uninhabited by humans. But what other predators might be out there? I asked myself.

The sun was reaching golden fingers into the river in front of me, waving and enticing me to enter.

I smiled, remembering Mouse once more, and then decided that the river had given me a good idea.

Any animal predators would find me more easily, even if I found a good place to hide and sleep, by my scent.

It struck me then – how much I'd changed in the last two years from who I used to be. As if the fires that consumed our house had destroyed her, too.

Here I was, on the first full day of being nineteen, at the edge of the river where I was about to bathe my body, miles away from that home that I'd seen burning just the morning before, and I thought of the bathroom where I had taken hundreds of baths over the past fourteen years.

I pictured myself at sixteen – that same summer when I'd gotten my driver's license, the same summer when Mouse and I worked at the ice cream shop together and hung out at the river every chance we could, and the same summer when the virus hit—getting into the bath one afternoon after work.

Each corner of the tub was stuffed with shampoos and conditioners, bubble baths, shaving creams, face cleansers – more than one of each, more than anyone ever really needed. Certainly more than I needed. But each little plastic bottle in their pastel colors somehow buoyed me – from the doubt and insecurity I felt when I saw influencers promising great results from the products, when I looked at their flawless skin and thin bodies and amazing hair.

When I used the products, I imagined that I was them. Beautiful like them. And the hot water and the myriad sweet fragrances and bubbles all over my body convinced me that this was true.

And then I saw myself getting out of the tub and facing dozens more plastic bottles and tubes and little square and rectangular boxes on the counter next to the sink. Pore reducer. Moisturizer. Buffing lotion. Setting spray. Eyebrow tweezers and eyebrow pencils. Mascara. Blushes. Literally dozens of shades of eye shadow.

I knew there were dozens more – not only in plastic but in glass and foil packets underneath the sink, too—the products I'd half used or grown bored with before moving on to better versions.

What had I been thinking? Who had that girl been who thought she needed so many oils and creams to be beautiful enough?

Wasteful. Selfish.

The anger I felt at who I used to be, though, ignited the rage I'd been holding back since the collapse: what kind of society had we lived in that made it acceptable for a perfectly beautiful sixteen-year-old to think she needed so many products to become a better version of herself?

And why hadn't any adults in the world been able to stop all that? Before it was too late.

I felt a burning in my heart as I compared who I'd been with who I had become. I saw clearly now how I had contributed to all the lavishness that led to the collapse. And I knew now how little I really needed to survive.

And inside me, all throughout me, burned a greater question that maybe this was all necessary, maybe it needed to happen, maybe nature devised a way to stop us in our tracks before we could destroy her?

This wild-haired, stinky thing I was, my body was, my soul was, here at the edge of the river: the truth was that I liked her more. I respected her. I knew what she'd been through and I'd seen how strong she'd become. How much beauty was in that strength that no product could give, and no collapse could take away.

So I looked around me on the riverbank once more, waited and listened, and silently undressed. The water was cold as I waded in, but it felt soothing to my muscles, especially those in my back and shoulders after a night of paddling, and I sighed as I floated, always keeping an eye on my backpack and swimming closer to the shore from time to time so I didn't lose track of it.

After my morning bath, I put on fresh socks and underwear and laced up my shoes but didn't dress completely. I took my t-shirt and shorts and dipped them in the river to clean them, too, and then hung them from a strap on my backpack after wringing them dry as best I could.

If I'd run into humans at that point, I would have looked like a recently submerged muskrat, wet and drippy and somewhat grumpy. But there was nothing I could do about it. My greatest need at that point was to find a suitable place to sleep.

I left the kayak where it was, taking note of the trees nearby – a copse of river birch and willow guarding the small sandy shore and circled by loblolly pines rising from the edge of the forest floor. And I started to walk.

The land rose gently up and was soft with last year's leaves and pine needles. Already the heat of the day was entering the shaded forest, and my own energy reserve was almost empty.

And then I heard it.

A gentle trickling.

Was I dreaming?

I followed the sound to my right and there it was: a tiny waterfall coming from higher ground and heading back toward the river.

I couldn't believe it. I pulled my water bottle out of my backpack and held it under the stream. Clear. Chilly. Miraculous. Water.

I sipped slowly, feeling my mouth and throat, and then my whole body, quenched with relief.

Water, like air, is easily taken for granted. Both, when withheld, cause great pain to the body. I'd felt this pain when I'd woken in my room filled with smoke the morning before, and I'd felt it at the river the day before when that guy stopped me from refilling my water bottle.

And fear stopped me, too – the fear of him, of what he'd done to that woman, of what he'd told me about the river being polluted. All this added up to make me mistrust the water.

But now, as my tongue turned from reptile to amphibian to fish in my mouth, happily evolving to swirl and swallow and quench my hot sorrow, I remembered that saying from a few years back when Native peoples were protesting the oil pipelines running through their rivers and lands: water is life.

And I was still, despite everything, alive.

This was a good place to stay and rest, I decided, once my belly was full of water and I could feel my arms and legs, hands and feet, every joint in my body soaking in the lubrication and sighing with relief.

I gathered up some dry leaves into my arms and arranged them around me as camouflage, then put my jacket over me like a blanket, and then my backpack -- with my last can of soup in it that I could eat when I woke up to prepare me for whatever came next – became a pillow beneath my head, and I fell gratefully, deeply asleep.

The peace did not last long.

At first, I thought I was dreaming.

The metallic sound reverberated through the trees from the direction of the river. I would have sworn it was a train but there hadn't been fuel for trains or cars or trucks in a very long time. Some kind of boat maybe?

I lay under the leaves that I hoped had become my hiding place and listened carefully. It was rhythmic like a train clacking upon tracks, but it was softer. It reminded me of something, and then I realized what it was: a waterfall. It sounded like my waterfall, but larger, and it was coming from the river.

My clothes were still damp, but I put them on anyway. Whatever this sound came from, it was most definitely human, and I wasn't about to encounter them almost naked.

I made my way back toward the river, moving slowly, standing behind one tree trunk after another to watch before proceeding. I wasn't about to make the same mistake I had near the river in the city again.

And then I saw it. It was like something I'd seen in a history book, or in movies about the past. It rose above the water, white like a wedding cake, and at the back was a waterfall.

Or more precisely, a wheel that created a waterfall so the steamboat could move down the river.

I couldn't believe it. But I didn't linger long on my amazement because I quickly realized this meant that the possibility of humans – enough humans to rehabilitate and manage a steamboat – was very real, even out here.

It was time to move. I turned from the tree that was concealing me and scrambled back the way I came, passing the waterfall and my sleeping place and following the stream as quickly as I could. I did this for two reasons: the waterway would provide a route for me back to my kayak when I was ready to return to it, and the sound of the water over rocks might be sufficient to mask the noise I was making as I ran through the woods.

Three reasons, actually: the creek would also provide me with fresh water. Once again, I realized how stupid I'd been in the past to take water for granted. Even now I was thirsty once more from the walking and running I'd done, and I couldn't wait to stop to drink more.

But there was no time for that now. I could still hear the steamboat in the distance, and I wanted to get as far away from the possibility of human contact as I could.

My clothes were damp, and I was sweating, and I was thirsty. Too much water on the outside of me and not enough on the inside made for a very uncomfortable body.

And I was also tired. And filled with anxiety. And hungry. And sore from a night of paddling down the river. And I'd been alone for so long. But I was so frightened of not being alone.

But mostly, as I ran as fast as I could beside the stream deeper into the forest, I was starting to admit to myself that I was really, really angry.

Chap

I slept well the next day, buoyed by a good night's work and the memory of my father and the water lessons he'd given me.

And the fact that my slumber hadn't been interrupted by humans as it had the day before.

When the sun began to tip down over the river, I woke in a generous mood, and said to my strongest son, "How would you like to examine the farthest dams with me?"

Henry's nose bounced happily as he asked, "Really?"

I could sense the jealousy coming from his brother, Mack, and sister, Gigi, but I told them, "Your turn will come soon enough. It's not safe to go with more than one of you at a time."

They nodded.

After a quick breakfast of duckweed in our pond with the orange sunset light emanating around us, Henry and I headed out through the nearest foraging canal. We followed this waterway that I'd built years before, leading from our pond to the next dam – a channel two feet wide and two feet deep – that enabled us to swim quickly, avoid predators, and forage.

As we approached the first dam, I was pleased to see that it looked good, strong, and sturdy, helping to create a pond on the other side of it where green plants could grow and flourish easily – more sweet greens for us to supplement our woody diet. But we did not do this for ourselves alone.

As I looked up into deepening dusk toward the trees along the bank of the pond, I could see dozens of bright white birds roosting among the dark branches of oak and ash. I knew that our pond also enabled the egrets to enjoy the food and water that made life possible there, and it made me happy that we could help to create a safe sleeping place for them, too.

I pointed this out to Henry so he could understand the larger importance of the work we did, and then we left the canal and waddled up onto the dam briefly so we could cross through that pond to keep heading closer to the river.

Along the farthest bank was a beautiful stand of willow trees - our favorite.

Henry and I paused there, and I showed him how to determine if a tree was old enough for harvesting.

"We want to let the young ones grow," I told him. "This ensures food for our future – and our future generations."

He wrinkled his nose at me, and I knew he wasn't ready yet to think about himself as a father of future generations. He was still too young, and his reproductive capacity wouldn't begin for two years more.

I showed him one tree that was old enough to be harvested but not so large that we couldn't finish it quickly and take it to a nearby cache on our way back.

"We don't want to waste anything," I said. He knew this already, and I knew that he'd heard it from me many times over. But this was a lesson that needed to be ingrained in the brain of a beaver. Otherwise, there was the danger that the balance of land and forest, river and water, would be upended.

It was important not to rush: this was one of the rules of the water way.

After I showed Henry how to bite into the wood in a methodical but careful way, I told him a story of what I'd been like when I was younger.

"I wasn't always as old as I am now," I said.

I saw his eyes crinkle slightly, but he dared not say anything.

"I was young like you once," I continued. "And I wanted things done yesterday. When your mother and I were first together, I was so eager to make a lodge for her that I processed the wood sloppily."

He paused in his chewing, opening his eyes widely.

"Do you know how soft and smooth the inner walls of our lodge are?"

He nodded, then continued to chew once again.

"Well, the first lodge I tried to make for your mother, I fit the pieces together as quickly as I could. I didn't pay attention to the smaller places that stuck out where branches had once been. I didn't think it was important. I wanted to focus on the big picture, not the tiny parts."

I noticed him slowing down his jaws as he listened.

"And the first night we went to rest in the lodge, the bottom and sides were like spikes all around us. She was patient with me and tried not to show it, but it was painful. We rolled and wiggled and tried to get comfortable. But it was impossible. We hardly slept that day. And the next night, I destroyed the whole thing."

He dropped a piece of willow into the pile next to him.

"I had to start over," I said. "When something is wrong from the beginning, that's the best thing to do."

Once I'd finished my story, I let myself appreciate the sweetness of the willow just underneath the bark as we chewed peacefully together, allowing the medicine of the tree to enter our bloodstreams and make our muscles, sore from nightly chopping and hauling, more relaxed. We were happy.

Once the willow fell and our bellies were full, we continued along the waterway. This time, we used a stream that had been there for many beavers before me. I didn't know this for myself firsthand, but I'd heard stories that this water came from many miles away, in something called mountains. My relatives had told me that the land rose far above them like clouds, and this is what made the water in this stream so clear and cold and sparkling.

The air trapped between our two layers of fur kept us warm and cozy, and we swam, using our tails as rudders to navigate quickly around the rocks that sprung up in the creek and gave it a bubbling, joyful nature.

The night was halfway over, and we had almost reached our farthest dam when I came up for air and smelled something.

"What is it?" Henry asked me.

"Quiet," I whispered to him, and floated with only my snout and eyes above the water so I could sniff and listen.

He paddled in place likewise beside me, watching me intently.

It was sour. And sweet. There was fear in it. And exhaustion. And something I hadn't smelled for a very long time.

"Let's go," I said. "But slowly. And quietly."

I could tell he was excited about the prospect of this adventure as I led him to the sandy bank beside the creek and we clambered onto land.

I walked in front of him, stopping every few feet to rise up on my hind legs, using my tail as a kickstand to balance myself, and pausing to make sure the coast was clear for the next leg of our lumbering land journey.

In this way, I was teaching him without telling him that the land was more dangerous to us than the water and that we must be as slow and deliberate here as we could be quick and instinctual in the water.

We'd gone about fifty yards when the scent became much stronger, and I knew Henry could smell it, too.

He moved his ears toward the sweet and sour heaviness. Did he hear it as I did?

I sensed he could.

A small and low breathing.

This creature was sleeping, his ears were telling him, and I watched the muscles on his back and shoulders begin to relax – just slightly. Beavers are never completely relaxed on land.

We let our front paws return to the ground again, and once more, I took the lead, heading in the direction of the scent and sound.

How long had it been since I had seen something like this? I was trying to remember while also keeping most of my mind energy focused on the possibility of other predators.

"Papa!" Henry chirped to me. He had gotten sight of the creature.

At this sound, her breathing shifted slightly, as her sleeping mind registered a change in the vibration of the forest around her.

I wrinkled my nose and shook my head at him, warning him to stay quiet and make no more vocalizations.

She was grown, but just barely. She reminded me of my kits in litters past when I'd encountered them after they'd left our lodge. But she was clearly not thriving as they had done.

She was thin. I could see the bones of her shoulders and elbows, even the bones of her knees and hips, seemingly trying to poke through the skin from the lack of blubber covering them.

Her hair was tangled and matted. I had a sudden urge to cut it away with my teeth, making it shorter so I could groom her. This impulse surprised me as I'd never before felt this kind of temptation to care for a human.

But she was so thin, and so disheveled, so obviously neglected, and hungry and alone.

Then she moved.

Her left arm, the one closest to us, rose above her body, and we froze.

She was near enough to us that if she had opened her eyes, she could have seen us.

I berated myself silently for bringing my son so close to a human. Especially a starved and exhausted human that could be dangerous.

But there was nothing we could do in that moment. To move and rustle even one leaf around us might have been enough to wake her.

Her left arm came slowly down, and she shifted her position. Fortunately, she did this with her eyes still closed, in a gesture that reminded me of my mate Penny and how she often turned over in her sleep.

As she settled into this new spot, I heard Henry's intake of breath at the same time that I noticed it, too.

Her breath caused her belly to rise and fall, and I thought of the mountains and the clouds and the rain that had given birth to the stream that we could still hear burbling in the distance behind us.

All things are connected like water, my father had taught me, and I knew that somehow, for some reason I could not discern at the moment, that this human was also connected to us.

Because what Henry and I could see clearly, what was obvious from the swell of her belly as it rose and fell with her sleeping breath: this human was holding within her body a soon-to-be newborn human kit.

Livia

I'd traveled deep enough into the forest that I felt safe letting myself sleep at night instead of catching naps during the day. But this was a mistake.

The first time I slept through the night, my body relaxed enough to allow me to dream. And those dreams were nightmares.

"I love you, Baby Girl," my mom mouthed to me from behind the large glass window in the oxygenated room where they'd put her – both as an attempt to fortify her deteriorating lungs and failing organs and to keep others from contracting the virus.

She smiled, her lips blue, and blinked at me, and then she was gone.

I relived that moment over and over in my sleep that night.

Each time, I awoke with a start, terrified all over again at being left completely alone, only to wake in the deep darkness of the woods around me with the confirmation that I was more alone than I could have ever imagined being on that day.

Except that I had not really been alone.

I rarely let myself think about it much over the course of the past eight months. My memory was somewhat like a broken window in a house that had been boarded up so long that it was easier to forget that there had ever been a view.

The first month had been the worst.

My body had been the broken window then.

It wasn't just the bruises on my thighs and back and cuts and scrapes on my arms and hands. It wasn't just the headaches that squeezed the sides of my head until tears came from my eyes if I didn't make myself lie down in a darkened room.

It was the constant stream of lightning coursing through my blood. The need to get up and move – rearrange the useless baking pans underneath the cold oven in the kitchen, go through the clothes left hanging in my mom's closet and arrange them by color, touching and sniffing each one to see if I could conjure her again, sweep the cold floors of the house with a broom over and over while letting the useless vacuum sit silently watching from the closet.

I would find any excuse to keep moving just to keep the strikes of lightning at bay.

But it still didn't work.

And so I walked. I told myself I was foraging. I had run out of the boxes of food I'd pilfered from a big box store during a night of looting, back when there was still gas available for our car and I'd told myself I wasn't stealing. I needed the food.

Forage. Pilfer. Loot. Steal. These words meant nothing anymore, not when everything had broken down.

But the truth was I was running from the storms inside me. The only time my mind and body calmed down enough for me to feel a slight resemblance of what I used to call calm was after I'd walked five miles or more to find food in abandoned homes and restaurants and stores.

And, just as the constant motion had allowed my nerves to settle back into balance, that first night of deep sleep in the forest brought back the full memory.

It was a dream but not a dream. A nightmare that I felt in my body. I felt the terror and the pain in a way I never had before.

It was December. It had turned cold. Of course, the heat in the house did not work because the electricity grid had been down for months, but we did have a fireplace.

So, heading out on one of my daily foraging trips, I decided to take the crosscut saw from the garage. I'd never done it myself, but on camping trips with Mom and Katrina and Mouse, I'd seen my mom cutting wood with it.

It barely fit into my backpack, and I don't know why, but the fact that I couldn't completely zip up the top so bothered me so much that I almost didn't go. A frisson of foreboding flooded through me.

But the windows of the house were frosted over, and I needed wood for a fire, so I ignored that feeling and I went ahead.

Walking warmed me, and it was a sunny day despite the cold, so the hour it took me to head to a the nearest state park was enjoyable.

I could have cut a tree closer to home. Of course, there were trees in our yard and in those of the houses in our neighborhood, but for some reason it didn't feel right to take them down. As if they were people who lived there. Now that hardly any actual people did.

Small pines surrounded the artificially dammed lake in the park, and I decided those would work well. They didn't burn the longest, but they ignited easily and were light to carry. I'd brought bungee cords and ropes and nets in my backpack, as well – more gear that Mom and Katrina had bought when they started fishing on a regular basis. My plan was to cut and process the pieces of wood there, and then devise a contraption for pulling the wood back home.

I never got that far.

I'd taken the saw out of my backpack and was holding it against the tree, trying to decide where to make the first cut when he came from behind and grabbed me.

He pushed me so hard I fell into the tree in front of me and the blade of the saw cut into my right hand as I grasped the earth to try to break my fall.

Then he dropped me completely, taking the front of his knee into the back of mine so I lost balance and toppled to the ground.

He turned me over, and the tree that I'd planned to cut watched as he did what he came to do to me.

There was not much pain after the first cut on my hand. I went kind of numb and lost sense of time. It seemed to last forever. I focused on the pinecones digging into my back, and the green pine needles waving overhead, and the sound of the lake lapping onto the shore nearby.

At some point, I lost consciousness, and when I awoke, I remembered his voice from far away saying he'd enjoyed that and would be back to find me again.

I turned on my side then, my ribs and arms and shoulders burning with a bone deep ache and vomited into the pieces of last year's pinecones beneath me.

I had no idea what time it was, but I knew it was long past noon from the low position of the sun in the sky, and I wanted to be home with a powerful yearning.

My mom and Katrina had told me about sex, and because Katrina was a professor of Biology, I probably knew a lot more about it than most girls my age did. But I'd never pictured my first time being anything like this. It had never even occurred to me as a possibility.

And now, I desperately wanted my mom to come get me. Pick me up in her car, wrap a blanket around me, and take me home. I wanted her to put me in a hot bath with lavender oil and Epsom salts, and turn up the heat in the house, and when I emerged from the water, warm and wrinkled and clean, serve me hot chocolate and sit next to me on the couch while I sipped it and cried.

I wanted her to take care of me.

But she couldn't. Because she was dead. Mouse and Katrina were dead, too. I didn't even know if any of the other kids at my high school or their parents had survived. Why, I cried, wiping the vomit from my cheeks, and spitting into the ground, was he still alive when they weren't?

Why was I?

All this came back to me in a half-awake way on that first night I slept on the forest floor, and when I woke the next morning, I saw pine trees above me in the lavender light, and I wondered if they knew what I'd remembered, too. I had seen a documentary once about how trees communicate through underground networks, and I felt that here, in the height of summer and over twenty miles from those other pine trees, that these much older, much higher trees knew me.

Knew what I'd been through. What I'd survived. And they cared about it. They cared for me.

I rubbed my belly.

"You're not alone," I said to her, relieved to be fully awake now. "We have the trees."

Chap

Henry and I left the human sleeping with her belly rising and falling like ripples on a pond and continued on our way. It was completely dark now, and we still had a dam to examine, and because it was summer, the nights were shorter, which meant we had to work faster and smarter than in the other seasons.

I don't know why – maybe it was the visitation from the two male humans I'd observed, or the presence of the sleeping female human – but I had a bad feeling about what Henry and I would find at the big dam. I wished I hadn't invited him to join me even before we arrived.

He wasn't sensing my apprehension, though. He was enjoying his first long outing with his father, and I sincerely hoped that I was wrong about what I was suspecting.

I wasn't wrong, though.

Even before we could see the dam, I heard the warning sound.

Water was rushing over the northern side of the dam. This meant destruction had happened.

I stopped.

"What's wrong?" Henry asked.

I shook my head. I had no words.

We dove into the pond and swam to inspect.

The southern side was fine. I saw the rocks at the bottom that had been placed there by beavers before me, so long ago I didn't even know their names. And above and between the rocks were twigs and sticks, buttressed by mud and placed carefully to allow the force of the current to do the work of keeping them in securely.

But the northern side was a different story.

The top of the dam was crushed in.

That happened sometimes when a large log crashed into it, and this kind of injury was fairly easily repairable.

But as we dove deeper to examine the lower portion of the dam, I knew that this had been no accident with a log or anything natural.

This was human.

The rocks themselves had been crushed. Pulverized. Turned to dust.

Only a human could inflict such damage.

"What happened, Papa?" Henry asked me with tears swelling in his round, brown eyes.

"Dynamite, I think," I said.

"What's that?"

"It's a kind of fire stick that humans use to destroy our dams."

"But why?"

I shook my head. There was really no reason that I could give him that was sufficient to explain the deep destructive tendencies that humans had.

I could have told him that sometimes they felt our dams were a nuisance. That they claimed dominion over the land – and over us – and were convinced that they could do whatever they wished. That they sometimes wanted power over the flow of water for their own drinking needs or that of their farm animals or fields of growing food. That sometimes they just didn't like the look of our ponds on what they considered to be their property. Or that sometimes our waterlands encroached upon their roads and buildings, and they felt the need to reclaim those areas from the water.

But none of this was true here – in a forest that was mostly swamp and had been for hundreds – thousands – of years. Here in what even the humans had designated as wilderness, an area for wildlife, a place to keep what was wild safe.

We were wild, according to the humans. And they were civilized. They even called the ones who constructed huge dams to stop the rivers "civil engineers."

But this was not civil.

This was destruction, pure and simple.

There was no reason for it other than the mysterious tendency in humankind to hurt others and destroy what was precious and valuable to them.

Henry and I bobbed above the water after looking at the damage below.

"What are we going to do, Papa?" he asked me.

And my answer was the answer of beavers for generations: "We are going to work as hard as we can tonight to repair it, and we are going to return night after night until it is complete."

He nodded. He was a good kit. Strong and capable. I was proud of him.

"We start with the rocks and boulders," I told him. "We will have to look on the land for any that survived the explosion. But we will also have to look for more. I'll show you how to roll them to the edge of the water with your front paws. Once you get them there, it'll be easier for you to carry them. We are stronger in water."

"Why do we start with rocks?" he asked. It wasn't insolence that made him ask the question. It was curiosity and a desire to understand. These are good qualities in a beaver.

"The water is heavy," I said. "It flows, so it can seem closer to air and light than land, but the truth is, it's incredibly heavy, and if we didn't start with heavy stones, the dam would collapse under the weight of the water."

He got the hang of rolling and then swimming with the rocks we found together, and once we got into a rhythm, the work was quite enjoyable, as work always is when done well and carefully.

We'd placed about six feet of a good, solid foundation on the bottom of the pond when the light began to glow in the east.

"We'd better head back home, Henry," I said to him. "We don't want to be too far from the lodge in daylight, and we've got quite a journey ahead of us."

I could tell he wanted to keep working, and it delighted me that he was such a hard worker, so eager, and I was glad all over again that he was my son.

"I'm proud of you. You did good work tonight," I told him.

"Thank you," he said, and we took one more look at our labor for the night before we left it for the day.

I said a silent wish that the humans didn't come back and destroy even more while we were away.

When we arrived at the spot by the waterfall where the female human had been sleeping, we saw that she was now awake and sitting up. Her head was tilted back, and she was looking overhead at the overstory of trees above her. And she was crying.

She made no sound, but as an expert on liquids of all kinds, I could smell the salty streams as they fell.

Henry crinkled his eyes at me in questions, but he made no sound, either. I gestured to him to follow me as we navigated a larger circle around her than we had before. After seeing the destruction at our largest dam, I was taking no chances with humans on that day.

By the time we arrived back at the lodge, the sun was creeping above the pond, and it seemed to be moving as slowly as I was, for I could barely keep my eyes open as I headed through the door of the lodge.

Penny could tell something had happened, but she could also see how exhausted we were, so she patted each of our backs and whispered, "Sleep well, my loves. I've gathered a big meal for you to eat when you wake."

Livia

It had been three days since I ate my last can of lentil soup. Fortunately, my mom had taught me how to look for wild berries that grew in the summer, and I'd discovered tart blackberries, sweet blueberries, and the rather tasteless partridge berries along the sunnier slopes of the forest. But I knew I couldn't live off fruit alone and I'd have to make some important decisions about my lack of provisions.

And soon.

I was feeling quite weak, and my stomach was rumbling.

I was in this perhaps delirious state of hunger when I heard voices.

I froze.

"This is better, isn't it?" I heard one say.

And then the other answered. "Much. Opening that dam will make for some mighty fine fishing now."

Fish. That sounded good.

But I knew that without a fishing pole or the means to make a fire, fish would be useless to me.

I heard my stomach grumble and complain so loudly that I thought for sure they'd heard me. My heart was beating quickly. It was decision time, and my body was going to make the decision for me.

"Hey," I said and waved my hand as casually as I could as I signaled my presence across from them on the bank of the pond.

As if it were the most natural thing in the world for a young woman to be out in the woods by herself. As if the world as we'd known it had not ended. As if the last thing I wanted to do wasn't to place my trust in two unknown men.

"Well, howdy!" the taller one shouted.

The shorter one was quiet. He turned to the tall one and then to me, and the look on his face told me he was the follower and looked to the other one to make decisions for him.

"Want to come and sit a spell?" the tall one asked. "You have to be quiet, though. We don't want to scare the fishes."

I nodded and made my way around the pond. Halfway there, I noticed that the stream was pouring through a gap in the bank. This must have been the dam they'd mentioned.

"I'm Rusty," the taller one said. "This is my son, Grayson."

Now that I was close to them, I noticed that the shorter one was not only shorter but much younger. Maybe my age or even a bit younger than me, I was guessing.

"You aren't going to ask?" Rusty said to me.

"Ask what?" I stammered. I had no idea what he was talking about.

"Why I didn't name my son Rustyson?" he said, chuckling.

I shook my head. It had been a very long time since I'd been around people. I seemed to have lost the habit for conversation.

"Tell her, son," Rusty said, tapping his son gently on the shoulder to encourage him.

Grayson looked at me, rolling his eyes slightly, and told me the punchline of the joke: "Because steel is gray before it gets rusty."

Rusty laughed and said, "Man, that never gets old. It would be illogical to call a young one rusty. Ain't that right?"

I nodded my head and tried to act normal. They'd given me their names, so it was time to give them mine. That much I'd remembered from human interactions.

"I'm Livia," I said, and sat down next to Grayson. "Pleased to meet you both."

"Go get her a pole, son," Rusty said. "She might as well earn her keep."

As I reached into the plastic bucket for a worm, I told them, "My mom taught me how to fish. It's been a long time, though."

"Oh, don't worry," Rusty said, handing me a hook. "You never get rusty." He chortled again.

I nodded, attached the worm, and tossed the line into the pond. Almost immediately, I got a bite.

"You're lucky," said Grayson quietly.

It had been a while since I'd thought so, but sitting next to him, I was beginning to think maybe my luck had turned.

"I guess so," I said, and started rolling the fish in.

"A yellow perch!" said Rusty. "That's a sweet fish!"

I could feel my mouth watering.

"It's been a while since you've eaten, hasn't it, little missy?" he asked me.

I nodded.

"Grayson, light the fire. No reason to make the young lady wait any longer."

Grayson took a lighter out of his pocket and ignited the leaves and pine straw at the bottom of the triangular pile of sticks they'd already constructed.

"Find a green stick to skewer the fish," Rusty said. "Did your mom show you how to do that?"

"She did," I said.

"Good woman," he said.

"She was," I replied.

I pulled down a small branch of a tulip poplar tree that felt supple and tore it away at the place where it connected to a larger branch. It was nice and green inside. Then I dipped it into the water and handed it to Rusty, who'd already deboned the fish, and watched as he wove the branch through it so it wouldn't fall off while it cooked. I watched closely as I figured I'd have to do this on my own soon.

Maybe six minutes later, Rusty served me this roasted fish on a sycamore leaf that was as large and flat as a plate.

And then with my fingers, I brought the first bite of fresh food I'd had in months into my mouth. The tulip poplar gave a slightly lemony taste to the fish, which flaked on my tongue like butter. I could feel my stomach reaching up to grab hold of the first swallow, and I sighed as it went down my throat.

Grayson smiled widely while watching me. It was the first time since I met him that he'd looked happy, and it occurred to me then that he had probably also known hunger as I had. And loss.

"So good," I murmured, my whole body wanting to be filled with the next bite.

Instead, I reached out to him and said, "Here. Have some."

He looked at his father, who nodded, and then Grayson reached out to take a piece from me.

It brought him such pleasure that I gathered two more sycamore leaves and divided the fish into three equal portions. I'd forgotten that the serving and sharing of food was such a large part of the satisfaction of a meal.

I sat with them through the rest of the morning, and it was more human interaction than I'd had in a very long time.

"I grew up in the country. Just across the river from the city to the west," Rusty said to me. "But it was a whole other world out there. So when things started falling apart, of course I knew how to fish and hunt and trap and such. At first, I didn't mind all that much."

He was venturing into telling me how it had been before for them, and I wasn't sure I was ready to hear it. I barely told my own story to myself. I kept my eyes on the spot in the water where the line entered as he continued to talk.

"Of course, my wife – Grayson's mama – she also had grown up near me, we had known each other since we were kids, and her mama had taught her how to preserve and can food. Each year, she had always put up hundreds of jars of jam and vegetables and pickles – ooh, son? you remember them bread and butter pickles?"

Grayson nodded, but he wasn't smiling like Rusty was.

"What I wouldn't give for just one little slice of your mama's bread and butter pickles right now!"

No one responded. Whether it was his age or his generally jovial composure that made him different than Grayson and me, I couldn't say. But it was clear that Grayson and I were not merrily heading down this memory lane with him. That much we already had in common.

"And key lime ice cream? You ever had that, Livia?" Rusty went on.

I shook my head but didn't look at him.

"We had a lime tree that Meg tended. She kept it outdoors in the summer and brought it into the dining room in the winter. Whole house smelled of it. And while she didn't get many limes from it, those she did get she'd use in a special key lime pie recipe. Some she'd make pies out of, using fresh eggs from our chickens, and the rest she'd make into an ice cream. Oh, man. I can taste it now. Nothing like a big bowl of key lime ice cream on a hot summer day!"

Grayson and I stayed quiet. Except for the rumbling of our almost empty stomachs, the only sound was the bird song far above us in the forest canopy.

"Your mama was a good woman," Rusty said quietly. I didn't know if it suddenly struck him that there would be no bread and butter pickles to go with any other fish we caught or no key lime anything for dessert afterwards, but his mood had shifted.

A dark grackle landed on the branch of the oak tree near us. And before we knew it, a whole bunch of them had landed and were chattering and squeaking around us.

"You know what a big group of them is called?" Rusty asked us.

We shook our heads.

"A plague."

The word scared us, and I think the noise of the birds also frightened the fish, too, because it was a while before any of us had another bite on our lines.

Finally, when the sun was high in the sky, after we had each eaten two more fish each and our bellies were full, they told me they were going to walk over to the dam to see if they needed to open it up even more. I told them I just wanted to sit and rest a bit.

And then I took that opportunity to reach into their supply box and put a spool of fishing line, a hook, and a small lighter into my backpack. I'd noticed that they had several lighters, and a fishing pole wouldn't fit, so I figured I was being fair in my filching.

They came back pretty quickly, and I was relieved that I hadn't hesitated very long to take what I needed.

Rusty said, "Yep, the beavers have already been building that dam back up. If we're going to keep this as a fishing hole, we'll need more explosives."

The word scared me.

"Explosives?" I asked.

"We found an abandoned fireworks store near the highway," Rusty said. "Makes a good substitute for dynamite. We took as much as we could carry, but we used it all up already. Want to head that way with us?"

I smiled, more from my relief that they were leaving than at the thought of heading to get some fireworks. I was feeling as if I'd had all the human company I could handle after the nightmares of memory I'd just had.

"No, thank you," I said, as politely as I could. I didn't want to anger them. "I thank you very kindly for your generosity with the fish, but I need to keep moving."

"Where are you going?" Grayson asked quietly. He seemed genuinely disappointed.

"I have an aunt who lives that way," I pointed in the opposite direction of the highway to make sure they knew I was headed another way. "She's expecting me."

"Oh, you have family!" Rusty said, and I could see that he really was concerned about me. "That's good! We all need family – especially these days."

I nodded, wishing it were really true.

"Here," he said, taking the last fish out of the cooler. "Take this to her. Compliments of Rusty and Grayson Buck. You tell her we hope she enjoys it."

I reached out my hands and felt a sliver of shame for stealing the fishing supplies from them when they were so kind and generous to me.

"I'll tell her," I lied, adding another thing to feel bad about to my list. "I certainly will."

I wrapped the fish in a few of the large sycamore leaves lying on the ground and tucked it into an outer pocket of my backpack.

"It was nice to meet you. Thank you very much for the fish," I said.

"You're mighty welcome," Rusty said, looking down briefly at my belly. "You take good care of yourself, you hear?"

I nodded and walked away.

Chap

I woke before the rest of the family a couple of evenings later and lay in the secure comfort of our lodge, sensing something was different.

I didn't hear human voices as I had before. And it wasn't the silence of birdsong that had alerted me before that. In fact, the birds were back, which told me that the fire had passed us by, probably stopped by the waterlands my family and I had created all around us.

It was a scent.

That sour and sweet scent that Henry and I had smelled on our way to the farthest dam.

It was here. Near our pond.

I rolled slowly away from Penny and the kits and slid down through the main entrance into the water below. Once in the water, I could feel better for vibrations of movement, but at first, nothing drew my attention.

I swam over to the edge of the pond where I heard crows conversing. They were birds who prided themselves on knowing the latest news and spreading it as clearly as they could with their loud caws, and this told me that whatever had woken me earlier might be ascertained if I headed in their direction.

Close to the edge of the water, near where the crows were calling, I poked my eyes and nose up above the water just beneath one of the cypress trees that the kits had felled and now made a good cover for me as it bobbed near the bank.

And there she was again.

The female human with the kit in her belly, sitting right there at the edge of our pond in the orange sunset light.

And then I sniffed another scent.

Fire.

But this time, it was not the acrid smell of a large fire, taking buildings and trees and animals into its mouth as it roared. This was a small fire. A bit wet. Mostly smoke.

The female human was roasting a fish at the edge of our pond.

And the sun was descending quickly.

And my family would soon be waking.

Was it possible that it was this human who had caused the destruction in our big dam? And what was she doing here now? Did she intend more ruin? I had so many questions.

But I had no time for pondering. I needed to make sure my family was safe.

As quickly as I could, I bolted back to the lodge.

"Penny," I rasped. "Come with me. Henry, Mack, and Gigi," I said to the kits, grinding my teeth slightly to let them know this was serious. "Stay here."

Penny and I dove into the water using our back entrance, and I led her to the far end of the pond, where we had less of a chance to be noticed by the human.

"Remember when I told you Henry and I saw a female human near the stream on the way to the big dam?" I asked her once we emerged near the opposite shore.

She nodded, crunching some green plants that floated on the surface of the water for her breakfast.

"Well, she is here," I told her.

"What do you mean?" she wheeled around, looking.

When the female human came into her view, I saw Penny's little ears turn as she watched and listened. I saw her nostrils twitching at the smell of the fish cooking, and I saw her copper-colored eyes crinkling as she assessed the situation.

Then she rolled closer to me in the water and whispered, "She has fire. That's not good."

I agreed.

"But we need to keep working on the big dam," she said.

I agreed again. If we let the dam stay as it was without building it up night after night, the hole in it would only grow larger and threaten all our waterlands.

"I could go by myself," I offered.

"Too dangerous," she chuffed. "If there's one human, there's bound to be more. She probably wasn't the one who destroyed the dam in the first place."

We floated with our bodies beneath the surface and our heads just above the water and watched the human as she ate the fish, taking small bites and pausing as if she were listening to the birds singing their evening thanksgiving song. There was something soft about her. Vulnerable.

Penny was right. Going to fix the big dam by myself not only would mean the work would be very slow going, but it also meant that I might encounter the destroyers all by myself.

"What if we waited until she leaves or falls asleep?" I offered. "And then we could go all together?"

She thought it over, pulling more green plants from the water's surface and chewing slowly.

"I think that's best," she said finally.

But we still had a family to feed. So as quietly as we could, we gathered strips of bark and twigs and sticks from the edge of the pond and dove back to the lodge to feed the kits.

Penny stayed with them while I made several more dives, bringing a big, sweet tulip poplar log to them on the last run once it was completely dark.

And then, as they ground through it together in the lodge, I waited to see what the human would do.

First, she took out something from her backpack. I sniffed and smelled wood. But this was unlike any wood I'd ever seen. It was very thin wood, gathered into sheets and bound together.

Next, she took out a stick. But it was not a stick of wood. I smelled plastic and metal and something else. A liquid.

And she began to use the liquid from the stick to make markings on the thin sheets of wood.

I did something similar when I used my yellowish brown castoreum to make markings on piles of mud to let other beavers know that this was my territory.

Was she marking her territory, too?

She did this marking for what seemed to me be a long time because I was impatient to get working on the repairs for the dam.

When she finished, she gathered some water from the pond in a clear bottle and drank deeply.

Then she lay down on her side, turned away from the water, and fell asleep.

I could hear the soft wheezing of her breath moving in and out of her nose and mouth. She sounded like my kits when they snored sweetly after a long night of chopping and gathering. I felt a pool of honey opening within me then as I watched her. She didn't seem to be much more mature than my kits after they had first left our lodge to find their own territories and make their own lodges and families.

And yet.

Here she was, right next to our pond, without a lodge of her own. Sleeping on the ground. Alone.

But not for long. I didn't know how much time she had to wait, but it seemed that her belly had grown even bigger in the past few days since I had seen her.

Her kit was coming soon.

Once I was sure that she was fast asleep, I headed back through our main entrance to the lodge to tell the family that we could commence with our fixing of the far dam. We worked through the night, and even though our time had been limited by the waiting for the human to fall asleep, we labored diligently, and the dam was completed before daybreak.

As we neared the entrance of the lodge once again, I motioned to Penny that I'd be in shortly. There was a memory that was coming to me that I wanted to ponder under the rosy clarity of time before the sunrise.

I'd been away from my parents' lodge for less than a year when I saw him.

That year between when beavers left their parents and our third year when we settled down to mate could be the most dangerous of our lives. My parents had warned me of this, and as a result, I moved slowly and was overly cautious.

That may have been what saved my life.

I saw the human. I saw that he was putting something metal into one of the ponds that my parents had constructed. I loved the sweetness of the duckweed in that pond, but I made a note to try to find another place for such a treat. Perhaps a part of me was also ashamed that I was still relying upon the ponds in my parents' territory.

That day, I saw the human and I decided to stay away.

But I did not go back to tell my parents.

Not right away.

Two nights went by, and guilt finally led me back. I meant to warn them. I decided to admit that I'd still been relying on their engineering for my food source, and despite my laziness, I wanted to keep them safe.

I was too late.

I found my mother crying on the bank of their lodge pond.

"Mother?" I asked quietly.

She was startled. It had been many moons since she had seen me.

"What's wrong?" I asked her.

"It's your father. He was caught in a drowning trap at the entrance to our outermost pond."

"Drowning trap? What's that?" I asked, my heart beating rapidly.

And she told me.

I heard and did not hear as the knowledge sliced into me like sharp metal.

"How will I feed the newborns all on my own without him?" my mother cried.

All this came back to me as I dove deep into the pond and caught a healthy fish in my paws. He was startled. Beavers were not fish eaters despite what humans throughout the ages have thought.

I explained to the fish, holding him gently in my front paws, that I was doing this for the human lady. She would wake with the coming of the light and she would be hungry. She had a baby on the way.

The small-mouthed bass opened his quite large mouth to say okay.

And then I left him near the circle of ashes that had held a fire the night before.

Livia

I woke long past sunrise, satiated by the three fish I'd had the day before, which was more fresh food than I'd had in months.

The pond was calm. I could tell it was mid-morning because I'd slept through the dawn birdsong that I'd heard every morning since coming to the forest, and now there was only the buzz of bees and whizz of dragonflies and mayflies. I'd even missed the worst of the morning mosquito activity. It was so quiet I could hear my own heartbeat.

I opened my journal and began to write again. I'd learned to make the most of a page in the past year, my handwriting growing increasingly smaller as time went on. Each day I recorded what I'd done and how I felt, and it made me somehow less lonely to feel that at least I had a companion in these sheets of former trees.

And then I felt a leap.

It startled me. It came from within. I put my left hand on my belly while the right one still held the pen.

"You enjoyed that fish, huh?" I asked her. And I smiled.

She responded with another little leap.

"Are you a daughter or a frog?" I chuckled.

And then I swear, the next thing I heard was a plop in the water. I looked up to see the circles of ripples waving out in all directions from the bank.

There was another. And another. I counted fourteen bullfrogs leaping into the water near the lily pads.

Something about their leaping took me back to the moment I first realized I'd missed several monthly bleedings. At first, I told myself that I wasn't eating enough to menstruate. Katrina had been very clear with Mouse and me about how female adolescence worked and had insisted that we eat sufficient calories to keep our hormones in balance and embrace the changes that were happening in our growing women's bodies.

"Your breasts, your curves, the cycles your body goes through," she'd told us when we were in middle school. "These are all beautiful changes. Your bodies have the capacity to create life. That is a sacred gift. You must never degrade yourself or allow others to make you feel bad about what the source of your power is."

I remembered my mom's face as she spoke. A mixture of awe and amusement splashed across her cheeks as she smiled at Katrina.

As embarrassing as it was to listen to Katrina's lessons, I would feel later that they helped me navigate the treacherous waters of the teen years with some modicum of acceptance and love for my body.

But not this. Not the realization that what had happened to me when I was trying to cut down that pine tree not only cut me down, too, but left me with something inside me.

It had been a thing to me, I admitted that now, watching the bullfrogs jumping in.

Once they were ensconced below the surface of the water and the pond returned to its placid state, I rubbed my belly again.

"Well, that was surely something," I said. And for the first time, I felt that she was no longer a thing inside me but a being on her way into the world. I looked forward to her arrival so she could witness these things with me.

I hadn't been able to feel this way when we were still in the house. All around me were reminders of what wasn't there anymore. The lack of electricity, heat, air conditioning, and a working refrigerator to store food – these were bad enough. But on every wall and bookshelf were pictures of me with my mom, and me with Mouse, and the three of us together with

Katrina, and so many smiling pictures of Katrina and my mom. It felt like I would be bringing someone into the world to be surrounded by ghosts.

"She's never coming back," I heard in the black of night.

I sat up in my bed and looked around.

"Who's there?"

No one.

I was seventeen and Mouse had been gone for a week.

After the ambulance drivers came to get her body, I went directly to my room and closed the door. Locked it. I would not leave. Refused to eat.

My mom and Katrina took turns, alone and together, knocking at my bedroom door and begging me to open it. Sometimes whispering. Other times yelling.

My mom, pressing her body against the wood so hard that I could hear the hinges shaking as she sobbed, "Please, Liv, I can't lose you, too."

And on the night of the seventh day – Monday would always be a mourning day for me after that, the day I lost Mouse, the day I knew she would never come back—a voice woke me in the night.

"She's never coming back?" I whispered to the dark.

The dark said, "Never."

I threw back the bed covers and put my bare feet against the floor. Walked to the door. Unlocked it. Turned the knob slowly, not wanting to scare my mom or Kat.

Except that there she was—my mom, sleeping right outside my bedroom in the hallway.

She jumped up and hugged me as soon as she saw me.

"Liv, Liv," she cried. "I was so scared."

"I'm back," I assured her.

But part of me had died with Mouse.

Out here, though, I was beginning to feel alive again. Well, that wasn't quite right, because I'd never felt this way before. It was as if every cell in me were calibrated to a higher octave. Part of it was the necessity of maintaining a sense of elevated alert, I knew, as much of my survival depended on protecting myself from both human and animal predators out here or even avoiding the simple accident of tripping when I walked through the woods.

But there was something else, too.

I felt seen. In a good way. The way I had when I was little and I was playing on the playground equipment at the park, and my mom was nearby, and even if her nose was in a book, I knew she was keeping her ears tuned to my movements and safety.

I wrote in my journal for a while longer, wrote about this, pondering all of this as I always had on the page, and then, just when I was about to go gather some berries for breakfast, I looked over to the fire pit from the night before.

Gleaming in the center was a yellow fish unlike any I'd ever seen in my life. Its scales were slightly striped in deep gold and light tan colors. And it was much bigger than the small fish I'd caught with Rusty and Grayson at the larger pond the day before.

How did it get there? Had Rusty and Grayson returned to give it to me? I didn't think so. I was sure I would have heard them. Even in my sleep, I had become like my mom, with my ears always listening.

I took my tulip poplar spears from last night's dinner and went to inspect the fish to try to determine how long it had been there and if it were still fresh and safe to eat. And as I did so, I realized that the ashes from the fire had heated it thoroughly enough that it was already smoked and ready to eat.

I looked out over the pond, half expecting the giver of the gift to be there in front of me.

"Thank you," I said out loud.

And before I picked up my knife to cut away the bones, I said to the fish, "Thank you, too."

I thought a lot about the past that day. I don't know if it was a full belly or the protein from the fish two days in a row or even just the peace of where I was on that little pond, but I felt ready to think about all that had happened.

I remembered clearly the first day I had been truly afraid.

Katrina came home earlier than usual from work one day in late spring and yelled as soon as she entered the front door, "Babe! Have you heard the news?" I knew she'd finished teaching for the semester, and I figured she had some new departmental drama to share with my mom.

My mom was in the kitchen making one of our favorite dinners – a vegan chili with beans and carrots and onions and tons of potatoes, spiced with a red powder we had gotten in Chimayó, New Mexico, on one of our yearly summer road trips.

"What's wrong?" my mom asked, holding the black ladle above the steaming pot.

"They've discovered another new virus. It sounds bad."

At first, they started talking more quietly. And then they stopped talking altogether and just hugged each other.

Katrina was a professor of Biology at the university, and she didn't get nervous very easily. She was comfortable with the gorier things in nature. For her to say something was bad meant that it was horrible.

I went on my phone to look up "new virus," and my stomach lurched as I scrolled through the headlines. I suddenly wasn't very hungry.

I remembered then how I forced myself to eat the chili that night.

And as I recorded all this for the first time in my journal while I sat next to the pond that day, I cried for the first time.

I cried for Katrina and how she'd tried to warn us.

I cried for my mom and her incessant optimism, how she'd criticized Katrina when she went out that very night to a big box store to stock up on canned foods, buying so much that we had to store it all in the garage.

I cried for Mouse who was the first to go.

I don't know why these earliest memories of the end came back to me then. It was as if a dam had broken, though, and my tears finally were able to flow.

I recalled how school never started again, how that school year ended and then in the fall, all the classes for my senior year were online, and how without Mouse, it seemed pointless to keep going anyhow.

How I stayed in my room and slept almost all the time.

How Katrina and my mom had the news on incessantly, too. Sometimes when I woke in the middle of the night, I could hear it, the infection rates and hospitalization statistics and death numbers, still blaring from Katrina's laptop between them in bed.

I wrote about all of this, those first awful months and how the speed with which the virus took one person after another left us all in a state of shock, and by the time I looked up from my journal, the sun had already dipped low over the other side of the pond.

I was exhausted. More than tired. Spent and empty. I was thirsty, but I didn't even have the energy to walk a few feet to the edge of the pond to fill my water bottle. I simply put my journal and pen back into my backpack and lay my head upon it, watching the sun filter through the green leaves and turn burnt orange as it descended.

I supposed it was time. I knew I'd have to deal with these feelings at some point, and the springing the little one in me had done that morning, and the fourteen frogs I'd counted jumping into the pond, and the leap of faith I felt I was finally making to begin to welcome her arrival – all of this may have been the signals my heart needed for me to dive in and begin to face it all.

Better it should happen before she arrives, I decided. And I felt every muscle in my body surrender to the exhaustion of grief.

My eyes closed. At the edge of my consciousness, I heard something splashing in the middle of the pond. I didn't even have enough strength to open my eyes to see. I was already mostly asleep.

Chap

I woke and Penny was gone. I slipped into the water and came up with more of a splash than I normally did and sniffed for her scent.

I noticed the human was still there, asleep just as she had been when I'd given her the fish that morning. I breathed in and twitched my nostrils as I floated in a circle, trying to detect where Penny had moved. The freshest smell was in the direction of the southern creek, so I started heading that way.

No sooner had I paddled to the mouth of the creek than I spotted her smooth soft figure swimming toward me underwater.

We met near a low-lying stone and snuggled into a crevice where the force of the stream could make its way easily around us.

"Where were you?" I asked. "I was worried. You know it's my job to wake first and make sure the coast is clear."

She whistled softly. "My dear," she said. "The protection of this family is not your job alone, and you know it."

I huffed and said, "I'm sorry. You're right. But where were you?"

"I went to check on the big dam to make sure it held during the day. The good news is that it did, and the better news is that I detected no scent of humans in the area since the last time we were there."

"That is good news," I sighed.

"But there's bad news, too," she replied, and pivoted her snout in the direction of our pond.

"What do you mean?" I asked. I had a sense that I knew what she was about to say, but I played innocent.

"Since when do we provide food for humans?" she said in a low growl.

I dipped my head into the water and rubbed the top of my head before emerging again.

"Penny, I don't know…" I started to say.

She was angry, and her words came out in a rumble.

"Have you forgotten what destruction they can wreak? You and I and our three yearlings just spent two whole nights repairing the big dam that enables all our ponds and waterways to be possible! And that's just the beginning of what humans are capable of demolishing!"

I hung my head as close as I could to the surface of the water without going under.

"You didn't have to see what I saw as a kit!" she smacked her tail against the water in warning that I should never live through what she did. I knew that just before it was time for her to leave her lodge, a huge yellow machine had come in and razed her whole family's pond, simply pushing it away before creating a large V-shaped concrete dam to make a deeper, more circular lake deemed to be a more suitable space for human homes.

"I'm sorry," I churred softly to her. "I know. I know. I'm sorry."

She sat grinding her teeth for a while, at first roughly and then the motion turned into a softer whirring.

We'd been still for much longer than we were accustomed at that time in the evening, so she glided downstream a bit and motioned me to follow.

"I needed to check on the big dam," she said finally, "because I can't have you heading there today."

"What do you mean?" I asked.

She flopped over on her back and let her belly rise above the surface.

"They're coming," she said, and turned her head toward me to nuzzle me.

Of course, I had known that she was carrying kits who were coming, but with the destruction of the dam and the arrival of the female human, it had somehow slipped my mind. What a fool I was.

Sometimes I wondered if I was a good partner simply because I was so lousy. I remembered the first lodge I'd built for Penny—how rushed and sloppy it was. How I admonished myself to try harder because of that early failure.

And I remembered the first time she told me that kits were on the way. My first reaction was panic, but I didn't show it that day. Or any day after. Maybe she knew this and loved me anyway.

Regardless, I was a hard worker partly because I was almost always in a state of constant fear that I was not measuring up.

The food cache I collected for the first litter was, even to this day, the largest I'd ever collected. It threatened to topple over onto our lodge, so high was it piled.

And the gathering of willow sticks I placed next to Penny was a work of art, each piece perfectly placed and measured in synchronous harmony.

I didn't know if she noticed. All I knew was that I loved her and I wanted to do my best for her.

Her. And the two little ones when they arrived – my heart opened, and I remembered my father as I saw their small circles of eyes blinking for the first time.

These six eyes – my partner, Penny's eyes, and the four eyes of our first two little ones, Midge and Chuck – these were the reasons I worked so hard. The reasons I never gave up. The lights that shone on the beaver I would become.

"Penny, you're right," I murmured to her. "You are the real leader of this family, and it was wrong of me to question your decision to check on the big dam. I'm sorry."

She accepted my apology by rolling over a few times in the water, stretching and splashing me.

"Alrighty then, Chap," she said. "It's time for you to get Gigi and Henry and Mack and keep them out of the lodge today. I won't be able to join you in gathering food for many nights, and we are behind on our chores already because of the repairs we had to make, so you all have a lot of work to do."

I nodded. Work was my joy, as it is for all in the water way, and she knew it.

I watched as she headed up to the bank to gather willow and pine chips to keep beside her in the lodge for later.

Our three kits squealed with delight when I told them what was happening that night, and the full moon overhead glowed upon our backs as we took our places on the other side of the pond from where the human was sleeping.

"What will the newborns be like?" Mack asked. He was the smallest of our kits, and I knew he anticipated the loss of his mother's attention.

"They'll mostly sleep and nurse at first," I answered him.

"Nurse?" he asked.

"They'll drink from Mama's body," I said.

All three of them froze and stared at me. Their eyes flamed yellow by the light of the moon.

"Oh, I forgot that you don't make memories until you are older. It happened to you, too," I explained.

"What happened?" Gigi asked. I could tell she was storing away the information for her own use as a female.

"The mother beaver's body makes milk to feed the newborn kits," I said. "They drink it from her body, and it nourishes them and allows her to feed them without chopping and gathering wood."

"Eww," said Henry.

"And you're saying we did that, too?" asked Mack.

"Yes, Mack."

"And one day I'll do that for my kits?" asked Gigi.

"Not for a while yet. But yes, one day you will do it, too."

"And the human?" Henry asked. "Will she feed her kits this way?"

I thought about it. "Well, human kits are called babies. And although I've never seen it for myself, my guess is that yes, she will do that, too."

"Will we see it?" Gigi asked. "Is she going to stay?"

"I don't know," I answered honestly. But something dawned upon me then, as clearly as the light shone from the moon fully overhead now. I remembered how fierce and strong Penny had been after the birth of each litter of kits. There was nothing she would not do to protect them, even before they were old enough to wean. It might not be such a bad thing to have a human mother in our vicinity who felt that way, either.

"Papa," Mack asked. "So we start out eating the milk from our mothers, right?"

"Yes."

"And then we start to eat the branches and twigs and water plants around us?"

"Of course."

"But do humans eat trees, too? What if there won't be enough trees for us to eat anymore now that she is here?"

I smiled. "No, Mack, humans don't eat trees." I reflected briefly, and silently, to myself that this was one of the few generous acts they had managed to do for us beavers.

"Oh, good," said Mack.

"They do eat fish, though," said Henry.

"Yuck!" squealed Gigi. "That's disgusting!"

I laughed. "Come on, now. We've spent way too much time talking. We've got work to do. We need to gather enough food to feed your mother for the next couple of weeks while she tends to the newborns. Everybody spread out and start harvesting, and when you've got a nice pile, take it directly to the food cache near the lodge."

"When will they be here, Papa?" Gigi asked. "I bet they will be so little and cute! I can't wait to see them!"

"It won't be long," I said. "They will probably be here by the morning. So we've got our work cut out for us."

"If only it were already cut!" Mack joked, and we all laughed as we headed to our separate trees to do our part to help Penny and the coming kits.

Livia

I woke in the middle of the night to a moon so bright I thought I was back in the world again and someone had turned on the light.

But as I rolled over and felt the leaves and soft earth beneath me, I realized I had made a mistake.

I had not really left the world behind.

The real world had been returned to me.

I lay there, listening to the bullfrogs near the south side of the pond singing their mating songs, a low and sonorous rhythm that sounded like a word. It felt to me like they were trying to communicate something to me. At first, I could not understand it. And then it came to me.

The word was peace.

Over and over, like those mantra meditations my mom and Katrina used to listen to in the morning while they sat on cushions in front of a lit candle right after they got out of bed.

But this was not a recording.

This was real.

The pond undulated with soft curves of white and dark underneath the light of the moon from time to time as a bullfrog found a mate, but the song went on.

I watched the moon for a while as I listened, and she seemed to be saying something to me, too.

But her message was not in sound or word. It was a feeling.

I found myself holding my hands across the fullness of my belly, and it was as if my body knew the feeling the moon was communicating before my mind did.

Fullness. Abundance. Satisfaction. Completion.

The moon was reassuring me that I had all I would need.

My mind bucked a bit at this, especially after all I'd been through, all I'd seen, all I'd lost – and I noticed my skeptical brain wanting details, plans, confirmations of dates and times and specifics.

I smiled and patted my belly and told my mind to hush as I simply let my body bathe in the soothing light.

And then another sound came in long and loud, just above me, from so close that I froze.

"Who cooks? Who cooks for you?"

I knew it was the call of the barred owl. I'd seen one here before, on a Mother's Day hike with my mom. It had been her favorite family activity – to haul us out to a state or national park and walk and walk until by the time we got back to the truck, a deep calm had descended over us.

The peace of the bullfrogs.

The plenitude of the full moon.

The power of the owl's call.

These had been what she'd wanted me to feel when she took me hiking when I was younger.

On another Mother's Day hike when Mouse and I were fifteen, Katrina turned back to us on the path, smiling, and said, "Girls, did I ever tell you about how your mom learned to fish?"

Mouse and I smiled back. Of course, we'd heard this story a million times. And we knew we were about to hear it again.

"Oh, please," my mom groaned. But she was happy. She wanted to hear the story again, too, I could tell.

"Well," Katrina said, walking along the path again. "Your mama was not really into nature when I first met her."

"That's not true!" she protested.

"Isabelle," Kat smiled. "You know it's true."

"I loved nature, though," my mom protested.

"Loving something and knowing it are two different things," Kat smiled. Then she continued with the story.

"We were friends then," she said. "Livia, you and Mouse were toddlers. And Oma was visiting. So I asked her if she would watch the two of you one morning while we went fishing."

I remembered. The sand cookies we made with Oma that day—I could still taste their soft, sweet crumbs on my tongue.

"I told Isabelle to come before dawn. I wanted to have time to drive out to my favorite fishing spot and get settled long before the sun came up. I thought no more about it. She wasn't usually late."

I saw my mom shaking her head and grinning, knowing what was coming next.

"The time came and went," Katrina continued. "I called her. No answer. I started to get worried. I thought about going over there to her. Oma said to be patient."

"That's not easy for you, Ma!" Mouse quipped.

"No, it's not," my mom agreed.

"Finally, y'all showed up. It was past dawn. The sun wasn't all the way up, but I was sure our day of fishing was down the drain."

"I wasn't that late," my mom chuckled.

"Whatever," Katrina laughed. "We left the two of you in the kitchen with Oma who had already measured all the ingredients for the cookies so the process would go more easily."

"Cookies!" Mouse cried. "Oh, how I love those cookies!"

"And here's the kicker," Katrina said, turning to look back again at us a few steps behind her on the path. "When we finally got to the fishing spot, I asked her. I said, 'Isabelle, why were you so late? Why do you look so tired?'"

She paused, as she always did during her lectures and storytelling, for dramatic effect.

"Your mama," Kat said, shaking her head and looking right at me. "You know what she said? She said she'd been up most of the night Googling."

We all laughed. We'd heard the punchline a thousand times, and each and every time, we laughed.

"She said she wanted to impress me with her fishing skills, so she'd stayed up Googling how to fish!"

My mom grabbed Katrina's arm and kissed her. "It worked, didn't it?" she teased her. "I had some mad fishing skills. I caught you!"

Mouse and I looked away and rolled our eyes, but we were smiling. We were used to their love by then. Actually, that's not quite right.

We loved their love.

It was their love that had brought me here.

After I'd missed a couple periods and felt unmistakably nauseated, I decided to go visit a friend of Katrina's and my mom's. We'd been to her home many times before, for potluck suppers and celebrations of the seasonal equinoxes and solstices.

She worked as a midwife, I knew, and I thought she might be able to help me.

I walked to her house on a night of a dark moon.

No lights were on inside, but that meant nothing now.

I knocked on her door and waited. Heard soft shuffling from within.

When she opened the door, I couldn't believe how thin and old she looked.

"Barbara?" I asked.

"Yes," she smiled. "Livia, is that you?"

"It's me."

"You're alive," she said, shaking her head. "Come in."

She lit a candle, and we sat at her kitchen table, and I had no words to say what had happened.

She knew, though.

"I can help you," she said, glancing gently at my belly.

I looked down. I remembered that my mom, always obsessed with language and the origin of things, had told me that the name Barbara means foreigner or stranger and is connected to the word barbarian.

I thought of this as I remembered the love between Katrina and my mom, and how even then, after so many rights and freedoms had been won, there were people who would say my moms were barbarians – outsiders, not quite people, but others to be ostracized and excluded.

"I don't know," I said softly to Barbara. "All of a sudden, I don't know."

She reached across the table and took my hand into hers. Her hand was thin and bony, but warm.

"It's your decision," she said. "That's the whole point."

I nodded. I had made my decision.

"It's just that she is," I said. "The only link I have left to my mother."

And Barbara held me as I sobbed in her arms.

"I feel your love now, Mom," I whispered out loud. I felt that she was listening.

The owl hooted again. "Who cooks? Who cooks for you?"

"I cook for me now," I answered. And I felt from somewhere deep within me that my mom was proud of me.

My eyes closed as the moon slipped lower into the west, and I thought I might fall asleep again when I heard a strange sound. It was a bit like the tapping of a woodpecker but softer. Not as loud. The pitch was higher. It was more of a scraping than a drumming.

I looked around the pond without moving. It wasn't that I didn't want to be seen. I didn't feel fear. Instinctively, I knew that it was my presence as a human that might scare whatever was there. And I didn't want to startle it in its home.

As profoundly as I'd felt cradled on that full moon night, I knew that this pond in the forest wasn't my home. At least, not mine alone. I was still a guest. A very grateful guest.

As my eyes focused on the direction the sound was coming from, I saw a short brown animal next to a tree. He was turning his head to the side and biting into the bark much the same way humans would eat corn. But instead of taking each bite into his mouth and chewing and swallowing it as we would with the sweet yellow kernels, he would stop short with his large front teeth and move his head slightly down to saw away the next piece.

In this way, he could create smooth, narrow strips of about eight to ten inches that he would then pile next to him on the ground.

As I saw his front teeth flash briefly in the moonlight, they shocked me with their bright orange color. This was definitely a beaver. I remembered this about them from a book about forest animals I'd had as a kid. But I'd never seen one in real life. Our local zoo had otters, but this was very different from that. He was chubbier, for one. And his fur was thicker. He looked like a stuffed animal when he paused from time to time to sit up on his hind legs and look around. I guessed he was checking for predators. And that what he would be most afraid of was me.

I breathed as quietly as I could, not wanting to scare him, and I stayed so still lying down on my side while watching him that my back and legs started to ache.

But I did not move.

And I was rewarded for my efforts by the next thing I saw.

As the beaver started to gather his pieces of wood in his little front paws, he paused and whistled. And suddenly from out of the shadows came three smaller beavers, each carrying similar stacks of wood. They waddled together the few feet from the trees to the eastern bank of the pond, so near to me that I could hear their tails scraping along the ground behind them.

And then they plopped into the water, and I could not see them until one of the smaller ones came close to the surface of the pond on the northern side, and the ripples extended all around until they stopped at a large mound piled with sticks and mud.

Their lodge! I had chosen to stay on a beaver pond! Something about this so delighted me that I laughed involuntarily and patted my belly.

"Maybe you're not a frog baby, after all," I whispered to her as she swam in my belly. "Maybe you're a beaver girl."

Chap

I saw her.

Of course, I did. I had not raised eight litters of kits – soon to be nine – on this pond without developing a keen sense of what might be watching and listening to my kits and me in the night.

In fact, it was my job each day at sunset to venture out and inspect the circumference of the pond before calling to the family that it was safe to leave the lodge.

And I'd known for a while that she was there. I'd told my kits that they could harvest nearby but not to get too close. I knew I was taking a risk by doing so. But she was so deeply asleep when we first started our work that night, I thought we would be safe.

I saw her eyes glowing in the moonlight as she watched me. Again, she reminded me so much of my kits just before they left to embark upon their own adventures creating their families. Our eyes were round like acorns and hers had more of a pecan shell shape, but I sensed we were the same in some deeper way beyond outline and appearance.

I could see in her eyes a wonder at the world and a desire to be part of it in some helpful way. In this, she seemed very much like a beaver to me.

So, I let her watch me work for a time. I was almost finished with what I'd wanted to gather from that tree anyway, and I didn't see any reason to stop. I really did enjoy finishing a job once I started it. That, too, is part of the water way: flowing to the end.

She made no moves while she watched me, and I could tell she was trying very hard not to frighten me in any way. I was pleased by this and trusted that my intuition about her had been correct.

When I was finished with my pile, though, I whistled to Henry, Mack, and Gigi that it was time to take our chips to the food cache. They responded as I'd taught them to – diving into the pond right away.

After we tucked our chips into the crevices of the cache so their mother would have enough to eat in the coming weeks, they chattered excitedly about whether the newborn kits had come yet.

"Dry yourself thoroughly," I reminded them as we squeezed the water out of our two coats of fur at the main entrance to the lodge before ascending further. "We don't want to risk a moldy bed for your brothers and sisters to start their lives upon."

They wiggled and stretched to wring all the water out of their heads and backs, bellies and haunches and feet. And then we climbed up.

"Not yet," Penny whispered, as we circled around her with questioning faces.

Her voice was strained, and Gigi could sense it, too.

"Does it hurt very much, Mama?" she asked.

"It's not so bad," Penny replied. "I have the pine and willow to help me."

"What does that do?" asked Henry.

I answered for Penny so she could keep all her energy focused on the task at hand.

"These trees hold medicine in them that alleviates our pain," I said. "Do you remember when Mack was struck by that falling tree in the spring?"

"Oh, do I ever!" cried Mack. "I thought at first my tail had been cut off!"

"Well, I gave you willow then to help with the pain," I reminded him.

We all looked down to see where the tail had healed and left a long scar.

"I certainly learned my lesson about harvesting a tree too close to someone else," Mack said, looking at Henry, whose tree it had been that had fallen before Henry could send the warning call.

I looked over at Penny and could see that all this chitter chatter was not doing her any favors in her labor, so I said to the kits, "Let's go back out and start to gather supper for tonight."

That was their favorite part of working because they knew that after that, sunrise would begin to signal an end to the night's exertions. They were still young enough that they looked forward to the completion of a task rather than finding joy in the undertaking itself.

This time I led them to the ground beyond the west side of the pond where there were some maples I'd been saving for a special occasion.

They quite squealed with delight as I showed the trees to them.

We fanned out so each of us had a tree to ourselves – not so far that one of us would be in danger of being spotted by a predator without alerting the others, and not so close that a tree might fall on one of us as it had on Mack that day.

The maple bark was soft, but it was the cambium just beneath it that we'd come for. There was a viscosity in it that very few trees had – except maybe pine, which was much more bitter.

I chewed slowly, gathering up a mouthful behind my front teeth to let the syrupy juices linger on my tongue. It was a sweet treat, and a sweet tree, and a sweet night, and a sweet life, indeed.

From time to time, we all stopped and stayed very still to listen for predators. I'd taught my kits to do this because when we were sawing or chopping or chewing, we couldn't hear much else, and a coyote or fox could sneak up on us then.

During one of these listening pauses when the moon was in the west above us, I heard the sound I'd heard eight times before. I swiveled my ears in the direction of the lodge, and I could tell that the others had heard it, too.

A soft mewing.

The newborns had arrived!
Gigi, Mack, and Henry did not move but waited for my signal.

"Have you had enough to eat?" I asked them.

"Yes, yes, of course!" they chittered excitedly.

"Okay, let's go meet the rest of the family!" I chortled.

We waddled as fast as we could from the maples to the bank and dove directly into the pond, our tails acting as rudders to guide the way.

We stopped as we always did to dry off, and as we entered the main room, we saw them.

Six babies!

We hadn't had such a large litter in years!

"Good job, Mama!" I exclaimed.

Penny smiled. "It's a lot of mouths to feed," she said.

"They're so cute!" Gigi purred.

"And so tiny!" Henry huffed.

"And so many!" Mack crooned.

We all laughed. There is no joy like those first moments of meeting the small new members of your family. It was worth all the long nights and hard work and toil we would do in the years to come to provide for them.

I crawled next to Penny and nuzzled my snout against the back of her head as she nursed the babies.

The yearlings snuggled together a short distance from us, wanting to give the babies space to wiggle and turn as they drank their first meal.

I could sense the cooler air outside signaling the beginning of dawn. No longer did the moon's white glow beam down through the breathing hole in the roof of the lodge. The light was more golden now, and brighter.

It was morning. Morning on the first day of life for my six newborn kits. There would be many mornings I would live with them after this one, and many more after that, I knew, when they would live on after I was gone. This is something we accept in the water way when we become parents: our children are meant to flow like water to shores far beyond our own.

But the knowledge of it in no way diminishes the deep and abiding joy of that first sunrise.

Livia

I woke the next morning to soft pats on my face and hands. It had been so long since my skin had felt touching that I kept my eyes closed for a moment to cherish it.

While other viruses were spread by droplets that entered human bodies through the air and we'd become accustomed to wearing masks to cover our mouths and noses, this new virus had been spread by skin-to-skin touch. It adhered to the surface of our skin, and through some mechanism of sweat and the warmth that our bodies created, the virus created a key to unlock the door of the normally protective skin to let it in.

So the world stopped touching.

Or at least, we tried not to touch. Even the thought of touch became associated with fear.

I could not remember the last time I hugged my mom. I remembered Katrina and my mom hugging in the kitchen on the day in May when Katrina told her about the new virus. I remembered sitting next to Mouse on the rock in the river later in the summer after that day – I think I could even remember how casually she touched my shoulder while we laughed about some boy from school. But when was the last time I had hugged my mom? It was probably something minor – or felt minor at the time – a goodnight hug that she'd initiated, and I grudgingly gave.

But these were not hands touching me now. They were raindrops falling on me. I knew it usually rained on the day after a full moon, but I hadn't been prepared.

I needed, I realized, to build a shelter.

With this thought, I also decided that this would be my home. This would be where I would raise my daughter. Beaver Girl.

I picked up my backpack and carried it over to a fallen log to tuck it as far underneath as I could to keep it dry. I piled sticks and leaves on the parts that were exposed so they wouldn't get wetter. And then I had an idea.

I decided to walk closer to the beaver lodge to inspect it and try to get some design ideas.

The ground was muddy and soft along the bank as the rain came down harder. I walked slowly, almost waddling, keeping my arms out to my sides for balance, amazed at how my much it seemed my belly had swelled even over the past few days.

All the fish I'd eaten, I guessed, had really allowed her to grow. And the fresh berries I'd picked. And the new way I'd felt while living here – a discovery of the beauty in going slow.

Part of the slowness was emotional, a kind of tenderness I'd touched in myself, but part of it, too, was physical. I found a spot on another fallen log on the north side of the pond and lowered my body to sit. My breath was heavy. The extra weight was a load on me.

I looked at the muddy mound rising in front of me in the middle of the pond water, and at first it didn't really give me any clues to its construction. I couldn't locate a door. There were certainly no windows. Eventually as the rain came down harder, I could see that sticks had been placed tightly together and plastered with mud that were becoming wet and wearing away slightly.

Mud. Sticks. Round. That was pretty much all I could gather from the architectural wisdom of the beavers. And then I saw a clue. As the temperature of the air dipped, there was a small puff rising from the top of the lodge. Smoke? No. Breath! An air hole!

I realized how ingenious this was and how it would serve to give them fresh air while at the same time keeping them warm when fall and winter came. I decided I'd seen as much as I could of their architectural plans without entering the water and I needed to get going on the construction of my own shelter.

I took advantage of a break in the rain and headed back to what I now considered my side of the pond. What had been hard ground only a day before had become mud that was thick and soupy all around me. Yes, indeed, from what I'd seen of how the beaver lodge was constructed, this was the perfect time to make a home.

I started with the fallen log where I'd left my backpack and used that as a brace for a wall. My plan was to take sticks and poke them into the ground behind the log so they would lean into the middle and create the first wall. This way, I thought, the log could become a kind of shelf inside the shelter for me to keep things above the ground.

But I needed another side. I looked around for another log nearby, but there wasn't one.

There was, though, a large cypress tree with a smooth trunk that stretched about five feet across at shoulder height. That might work.

I hadn't eaten breakfast, but I was excited at the prospect of my new project, and the adrenaline of deciding to make this my home fueled me. I began gathering branches from trees, using my knife to whittle them away from the crooks where they met the trunks. I figured using green wood like this would make the construction sturdier.

I chose ones that would be long enough to reach from the log to the cypress tree, planning to make a sort of leaning tower with them. I quickly realized that my original vision for a shelf inside the house was not as important as the leverage the log would give all the branches if it were outside the house, so I began digging the branches into the crevice on the other side of the log where I'd hidden my backpack earlier. Sometimes I used my knife to make the ends of branches sharper, like spears, so I could post them more deeply into the damp soil beneath the log.

The branches that reached the center of the cypress held nicely, but this only gave me a width of about two and a half feet.

I sat down to think.

I wanted to take advantage of the wet mud to plaster the cracks between the branches as the beavers had done, so I had to work quickly. But I could barely fit into the space beneath the leaning wall I'd constructed. And I would need room for two soon.

I looked around at all the trees. For a second, I considered trying to go back to my house to get the crosscut saw again, and then I shook my head at the foolishness of that idea. That saw had not been my friend. And of course, I had no idea how much damage the fire had done to the city. The house was probably not even standing.

But I could still stand. So I did. And started walking.

What I discovered as I walked around the perimeter of the pond was that the beavers had felled more than enough trees for me. I could see the teeth marks that created fine sculptures at the base of the trees where they'd chopped nightly, and when each point was fine enough, the trees had toppled over on their own.

Most of the trees fell in the direction of the pond, and quite a few of these had their top canopies almost submerged completely in the water. But those that had fallen in the other direction caught my attention.

I went over to one, bent down, and tried to pick it up, squatting and bracing myself for it to be incredibly heavy. To my shock, it wasn't. I realized the time that had elapsed since the felling of the tree had helped to dry the wood and made it lighter. I wondered if this was why the beavers left them lying like that for so long – so they would be easier to carry later. And maybe this was a lesson in patience for me.

I looked over to the lodge and nodded a silent thank you to my neighbors, who already felt like friends of mine, more generous than any human.

I carried one log back to my shelter area and laid it down next to the base of the large cypress, nestled between two small roots that rose from the ground like knees. Ingenious, I cried! Even the roots of the cypress were helping me in the construction.

Now that I had a clear vision and a workable plan, I let myself take a break to eat. I picked up my fishing pole – just a branch that I'd tied my fishing wire to – and wrapped the hook to the other end. Then I dug into the dirt with my knife until I found a small shell. I'd learned that if I crushed the shell against a rock, I could make the soft body of the snail come out and pierce it with the hook to make a nice bait.

I smiled to myself. I was a long way from that seventeen-year-old I'd once been who drove too fast with the music so loud that she couldn't hear the traffic around her as she headed to the mall because couldn't wait to spend her babysitting money on lip gloss and eye shadow and the latest products that promised greater beauty.

It didn't take long. The fish loved these snails or mollusks – Katrina would be disappointed in me for not knowing precisely – but whatever they were, the fishes apparently found them delicious, and since they couldn't get at them themselves without hands or rocks or teeth enough to crush the shells, they immediately came swarming over to take a bite.

I caught another one of the big yellow ones that had been smoked in the ashes of my fire on the first morning I woke there, and then I collected leaves from the areas underneath the thickest trees that were still dry enough to start a fire. It was mostly smoke at first, but then I added a fallen branch of pine, and the dry auburn needles helped the flames shoot up higher. I deboned the fish, thanking it as I did so, and held a green branch of skewer over the heat until it was crisp and juicy.

Once I was finished with my lunch, I headed back up to the hilly embankment on the eastern side of the pond that I'd claimed as my own and began my building in earnest. I started by creating a triangular shape at the base of the cypress with piled logs to form two fairly straight walls, buttressed by the trunk and the roots below. And on top of these, I placed more branches that stretched across at a downward slope to the outer edges of my foundation log below.

In this way, two walls that formed an L-shape with the cypress and a nice, snug roof woven with sticks and drying mud were completed by the time the day signaled its ending by the position of the sun glowing above the western side of the pond.

I decided I was done for the day, too. It was still summer, and it would be too hot inside the shelter if I added the other walls right away. As it was, I would have the nice breeze that rolled over the pond from west to east most days that would flow over me as I slept or rested or wrote in my journal while I was in the shelter. It had been a good day. I had accomplished what I set out to do: create protection from the rain.

I had a home once again.

Chap

At sundown, I left Penny and our nine – nine! - kits still sleeping and went out to do my daily ritual of swimming around the pond to check for predators and keep an eye on the condition of the lodge.

I smelled in the air that it had rained that day, which had softened some of the clay on the roof and sides of the lodge. That would have to be repaired immediately.

Otherwise, everything seemed in order. No scents of predators or vibrations of visitors.

And then I saw her. She was still here. And there was more. She had constructed a shelter. I recognized some of the logs we'd harvested on the south side of the pond that had been drying since the early spring. I'd planned to use them for further bolstering of the lodge before the cold weather came.

It certainly was no engineering marvel, but I had to admire the ingenuity of this young human to take the materials we'd given – even though we hadn't meant to – to construct her lodge.

It must have been the rain, I decided, as I munched on some lily leaves near the bank and noticed the deep black color of the mud near the water, that triggered her desire for shelter. Much as the colder air would inspire a renewed interest in our own shelter when the seasons turned.

Would she still be here then? I wondered. How long did she plan on staying?

And then, as if she had heard my questions out loud, she suddenly looked up from the scratching she was doing on her tree sheets and looked at me.

I'd only ever seen her eyes in the night, but the sun had not yet completely set, so I could make out the color and depth of them now.

Her eyes had specks of gold like the sun in them, but mostly they were the green and brown color of our pond water. They reminded me of the reflections the leaves of the trees made on the surface of the water on days that were clear and warm and calm.

She was calm. I could tell that she meant me no harm. It is very difficult for humans not to move, I'd learned over my lifetime. They have an endless urge to make and go and do something. Mostly this doing was a form of destroying.

But I could see how carefully she tried to keep still as she looked at me. Even her large belly hardly rose and fell as she breathed. I mirrored this tranquility back to her as I floated in the water and stopped chewing my green leaves, holding them in front of me in my small paws.

"I'm Livia," she whispered, and my ears turned toward the sound.

She was giving me her name. I knew that this was how all creatures, bird and fish and animal, introduced themselves when they wanted to be friends.

"I'm Chap," I churred.

She grinned widely.

"Pleased to meet you," she said, still whispering, careful not to frighten me.

Maybe she wouldn't be such a bad neighbor to have after all.

Then my ears swiveled in another direction as I heard the soft and squeaky sounds of the waking newborns mewling in the lodge. She heard it, too, I could tell, as she turned her head in that direction.

She squinted, trying to figure out what the noise was.

I had no more time for chit chat, though, and I rolled onto my belly in the water to collect as many greens as I could for Penny's breakfast.

As I squeezed myself dry at the main entrance and shook out the water from the greens, I could hear all nine kits inside chattering. It was naming time.

I offered the greens to Penny and nuzzled the top of her head. The news about our new neighbor's shelter would have to wait until later, I decided.

"Papa!" Henry cried when he saw me. "We were thinking. Since there are three of us and six of them, maybe each of us could name two of them!"

I looked at Penny and she nodded, munching hungrily at her breakfast greens. Her eyes were soft, and she was tired but happy.

"Naming is a big responsibility," I said. "It is the word that will introduce you to the world everywhere you go. It tells others who you are."

Gigi nodded, smoothing the already thick fur on the backs of the two newborn girl kits she'd decided would be the ones for her to name.

Mack held back a little. I could tell he was saddened not to be the smallest one with the most of his mother's attention anymore.

"Mack," I said. "Would you like to have the honor of being the first one to give names?"

He grinned and puffed out his chest a bit. "Thank you, Papa," he said.

Then he picked the smallest kit and brushed his nose against him.

"You're the smallest," he said. "I know what that's like. So I will give you a name like mine and we will be best buddies forever. Your name is Mick."

"Mick and Mack!" Henry laughed. "I love it!"

Then Mack chose a girl kit and said, "You will be Meadow. You are calm and peaceful like the meadows I've been to where Papa told me our ancestors had ponds in the past."

"That's beautiful, Mack," murmured Penny.

"Thank you, Mama."

Next it was Gigi's turn. As the largest, Henry would be last so we could teach him the water way principle that with great strength should come greater patience.

Gigi snuggled against the two girl kits she'd already claimed as hers to name and said, "These two are always next to each other, I've noticed. So I've decided to give them names that match, too."

I could tell that she would be a good mother from the gentle way she smoothed down the larger one's fur as she said, "You are the biggest girl in the litter and there is a great composure about you. So your name is Gaia."

Penny nodded approvingly.

"And you are smaller but your coat glistens so beautifully," she said as she scratched behind the left ear of the other one. "So you are Gem."

"That's perfect," I said and gave her a little kiss on her head. "Well, Henry, you've waited patiently. Have you chosen your names?"

"Yes, Papa," he said. "I have the two biggest boy kits to name – like me," he smiled. "And like Mack and Gigi, I would like to choose a sound for their names that resembles mine."

I nodded. It seemed only fitting.

"But instead of choosing names that go with how they look, I decided to give them names that will reflect who they will be."

He was always the deepest thinker, my Henry.

"Their names are Hero and Happy."

Gigi laughed. "What great names, Henry!" she chittered.

"Thank you," he said.

"But who is who?" Mack asked.

"Hero is the one with that long, dark stripe on his back," Henry said. "It reminds me of the great lines on the bark of the largest trees in the forest. That's why he will be a hero."

Penny closed her eyes briefly, tears of joy swelling from her eyes, just as moved during this ninth time of the rite of naming as she had been during our first one.

"And this one has little lines around his mouth like he's already smiling," Henry continued. "That's why he's happy."

And indeed, Happy was happy. As were we all: one big beaver family snuggled safely in our lodge on that jubilant day of the naming ceremony.

Livia

I'd worked so hard that day that it felt like every muscle in my body had been pounded by wood, and yet I could not sleep that night.

The moon rose late but still mostly full in the east, and I watched its glow ascending through the shadows of the forest trees from the new protection of my shelter.

When it was directly overhead, I was pleased to see that I was still covered in darkness, so well had I patched the areas between the branches above me with wet mud that by now had now dried into a strong plaster roof.

Except for the small hole I kept at the top, inspired by the beavers' ingenuity, which would allow me a breathing space when the walls on all the sides were installed for the winter. Through this hole I felt the moon peer down on me in a soothing band of light.

And then she tipped west toward the pond, and I had a perfect view of her conversing with water for the rest of the night.

Together, her white lantern and the pond's silvery glow created the stage lighting for me over the area near the lily pads where the bullfrogs sang their nightly chorus. The show was joined by percussion section of crickets, invigorated by the morning's rain the day before.

I heard the owl again, too, this time from the direction of the north where they beavers' lodge was. And to my surprise, her call was answered by another one directly across the pond in the south.

I felt like they were calling me into the pond. And I stood up to answer their call. I took off my clothes and walked to the edge of the water. I'd never before entered it, even though I ate from it and drank from it and wrote next to it and slept beside it every day and night.

But tonight, with the moon glowing large above it, I moved into it with my equally large round belly shining in the moonlight in front of me.

The water was surprisingly warm and soft and welcomed me, skin to skin, like a friend. Like a mother. And I dove in.

As I held my breath and swam deeper, I felt something ignite within me. A fire. A burning anger. I wanted to scream. It threatened to drown me if I did not let it out.

So I came up, and I took a breath, and I dove down again. And I screamed. I screamed and shrieked like Mouse and I had done when we were girls at the pool in the summer, playfully experimenting with the sounds our bodies made under water.

But this was no play.

This was rage.

Why wasn't Mouse with me anymore? Why did I have to go through everything so alone? Why did my mother die? Why couldn't Katrina have saved us? Why did that guy live when they didn't? Why did I?

There were no answers to my questions, no reason for why any of it had happened, and this infuriated me further. I screamed and screamed the question anyway, coming up again to fill my lungs with air and fire and diving back down again to release my rage from the deep earth of my body into the willing water.

"Why? Why? Why? Why?"

Eventually, the firestorm subsided in me, as it had upon the earth in the days after I'd fled my home and city.

I was spent. Drained. Wiped. Wrung out.

As I emerged from the water, I was greeted by an amazing sight – the beaver I'd given my name to the night before was sitting right in front of my shelter and next to him was a small pile of soft branches from a willow tree.

I moved extremely slowly around him, trying to show him I was friendly, as I went to lie down in the shelter. Attempting to indicate that I would do him no harm, I did not look directly at him once I lay down but lowered my gaze to my belly that seemed somehow to have grown even larger during all my screaming and swimming.

What did he think of me? Did he think I was crazy? I laughed at the absurdity—but also the absolute truth—of the fact that I did actually care what this beaver thought of me.

With his little front paws, he picked up the six branches that were thin and long, about fifteen inches each, and bent softly down to the ground as he placed them in his mouth to waddle closer to me in my shelter. I could not believe what I was seeing.

For a moment, I wondered if he meant to use them as weapons against me, but no such worry was necessary, for he dropped the pile about a foot away from me and backed up slightly and seemed to bow, still facing me.

And then he spoke. It was a soft nasal murmuring, kind and almost cooing in its tone. He went on and on, sometimes whistling a bit through his teeth, sometimes chattering as he paused in his vocalizations and ground his teeth together as if thinking about what he wanted to say next. Or waiting for me to ponder his meaning.

The bullfrogs were listening, too—and the crickets and the night owls – as they became very quiet.

All the while, he was balanced on his hind legs and the kickstand of his tail, and he held his two little front paws below his chin. He had five little claws that curved out from the pads of his paws like fingers and glowed yellow in the moonlight. They looked so much like human hands.

Something about it moved me so that I felt tears welling up in my eyes. I wished so dearly that I knew what he was saying for I felt there was some message that would serve me well in the time to come. There was an urgency, an earnestness, and an eager helpfulness to his manner.

And then, just as the moon stood directly across the pond from me with the beaver in between -- creating a long, low shadow that touched my body, I felt the first wave.

It was as if someone lay behind me, arms around me, and squeezed my middle. I felt whatever this was as it turned the muscles of my belly from flesh to wood, creating a hardening that swept from my sternum to my inner thighs.

It was happening!

Suddenly I felt a warm gush between my legs. Katrina had taught Mouse and me when we were in middle school about reproduction, and pregnancy, and birth – partly to warn us of the very real consequences of our potential sexual behavior. But also because, I knew, she found the whole thing to be a miracle and a wonder.

So I knew now that this warm liquid running down my thighs meant my water had broken and labor was commencing. Oh, how I longed for the presence of my mother or Katrina or any companion then.

And at the same time, while I'd been distracted by the things happening inside me, the beaver had moved closer to me and was placing one small paw on my right shoulder as I lay on my side.

It was the first touch from anything alive that I'd felt since the night that Barbara held me after I made the decision that brought me to this moment and the imminent arrival of my beaver girl.

My tears were flowing steadily now, mostly from missing my mother and the rage and grief I'd finally been able to release in the water – but also from the incredible warmth and comfort emanating throughout my whole body from the beaver's touch – not to mention the titanic waves of pain that came like water and washed like king tides upon the shore of my belly.

I talked to my mother then, as my heart opened with love for her and for all she had given me. How I missed her so. Katrina, too.

"I am so sad," I said out loud. "So sad you are not here with me. How much you would have loved to see this. What beautiful teachers you were to me," I said and paused then because the tears were flowing so forcefully from me that I could not speak. Finally, I continued. It felt like a prayer I had to finish to prepare me for what was to come.

"Thank you for your love, and your lessons, and the belief you had in me all my life. Without you, without all of that, I would have never made it to this point."

In that moment, I knew their memory would give me the strength and wisdom to do what I had to do for my baby.

When the beaver saw me sobbing, he reached back to his pile of sticks and silently, slowly, took one and gestured as if he were going to put it in his mouth, miming a biting motion, and then placed it gently into my mouth.

I bit down and the simple action of having something between my teeth lessened the pain. My tongue and teeth caused the wood to become soft and pulpy, and a slightly bitter juice filled my mouth. But instead of spitting it out, I swallowed.

I remembered nights when I'd been a young girl and sparked a sharp fever, how my mom would sit on the side of my bed and hand me a pill to ease the pain, and then offer me a cool drink of water. This felt like that was happening again.

Except that I was becoming the mother now.

The beaver brought the rest of the sticks from the pile and lay them close by me, and one after another, I chewed on them and ingested the healing juices while the moon, large and low on the western horizon over the water of the pond, continued to watch as wave after wave of pain and hardening and loosening crashed upon my body. I knew how to surf these waves because of the earlier experience I'd had swimming in the water: Surface. Breathe in. Dive. Vocalize. Let go. Repeat.

Then I'd been surrendering to rage and grief. Now I was freeing into life.

Then the pond became very quiet.

I took a deep breath, as if I were going to dive to the bottom of the water and dig into the mud below and would not be able to breathe air again for a very long time, and I held it within me as I counted to six, seven, eight – all the way to nineteen, the number of years I was right then – my energy gathering and rising within me.

And then a great shaking ran through me and every muscle in my body participated in the movement as my baby entered the world through my legs and onto the soft floor of our shelter, as oak leaves and pine needles and cypress fronds became the first contact the skin of her body had with the earth.

I cried with joy to see her here with me after all we had been through together.

I sat up slightly and reached into my backpack for my knife to cut the cord connecting us. I hoped it didn't hurt her.

I brought her up to my chest, both of my arms cradling her wet warmth and noticing the soft white cream on her skin that had served as a kind of lotion while she'd been growing in the pond of my body. Vernix. Mom and Katrina had even taught Mouse and me the word for this as they told us our birth stories.

The beaver was still beside me, and he placed the final stick into my mouth as another wave of pain hit, and out came the rest of the cord connected to the placenta, which looked like a deep purple eggplant. This had been her shelter, and now she had me and the shelter I'd built that very day to protect her.

What a day it had been. Some days are like this, I learned then. They take whole lifetimes to understand. They change whole lives and the generations to come.

The baby was crying now, a rhythmic, desperate cry that reminded me of my own sobbing earlier in the water, and as I held her, I understood what it felt like to have to leave one world and enter another.

Eventually, her cries turned softer, and she began to coo and grunt a bit, nuzzling at my chest, and another, softer wave flowed through my breasts as I felt them harden and watched as they produced thick yellow drops of liquid. How much my body knew what to do!

I placed her mouth on my nipple and she did not suck exactly but kind of kissed the area and licked the sweet liquid with her lips.

I remembered when we'd had a hamster when I was very young, and my mother had to give her some medicine once and squeezed his cheeks so his mouth formed a circle so he would drink from the syringe.

I did this with the baby's cheeks as she pressed her lips against me, and it worked. She was drinking from my body!

The beaver chortled beside me.

I laughed, too.

She was really here. My baby. My Beaver Girl.

Chap

It had been Penny who sensed what was coming.

About halfway through the night before, when the moon was directly overhead and glowed through the top of our roof, Penny thanked me for a delivery of lily pad roots as she nursed the six kits – Mick and Meadow, Gaia and Gem, and Hero and Happy – each of them only a little over a day old and already showing their own distinct personalities.

"Chap," she said softly. "Livia's baby will come tonight."

I did not know how she knew this, but I remembered that all our litters had also come near the time of the full moon, so I did not doubt her.

But what she said next shocked me.

"Chap, you have to help her."

I cocked my head and asked, "How?"

"Gather the willow for her. It will help her with the pain as it does for us."

I hadn't known this – that our bodies were so like the humans.

"And stay with her," Penny continued. "She's young. And she's alone."

I nodded and kissed her before I went to gather willow and complete my task.

But as I swam through the water and saw her, bobbing down and bouncing back up, heaving air into her lungs, and screaming again and again, I realized that this was not just a simple chore I was doing.

There was a deeper solemnity to it.

What Penny had asked me to do was something beyond what I'd ever done for anyone – even Penny herself, who'd birthed all our kits on her own.

I emerged from the water and collected the willow, then waddled on land around the pond so as not to disturb her in the water and put the pile of willow sticks on the ground next to me as I waited for her.

When she finally emerged from the water and saw me, she moved slowly and respectfully around me, and then lay down in her shelter. I gathered the willow branches and brought them closer to her. Then I began to speak.

"I'm Chap. I don't know if you remember. Your name is Livia. I remember that. It's a nice name. We just had a naming ceremony for our newborn kits. There are six of them. That's the biggest litter we've had in a long time. My partner Penny and I, and our yearlings, too, have seen that you are carrying new life."

I paused.

"Anyway, I was thinking about your name. It's a nice name. It has the word 'live' in it. That's good medicine. It's been a bad time for everyone – humans and beavers and even the birds and the trees have suffered. That fire was terrifying, wasn't it? Was that what brought you to us?"

I waited to see if she might answer. She was listening so intently.

"Well, it doesn't matter how you got here. Because you're here now. And my partner and I want you to know that we consider you part of our family. We've lived on this pond for a long time. Maybe as long as you've been alive. And of course, we chose this spot because of its lack of proximity to humans. But you're here now."

I saw her close her eyes and wince as a wave of pain came through her body. I took a chance and moved closer, and then I laid one paw softly upon her shoulder.

Her eyes grew wide, and again I saw the gold and green and brown sparks in them, like the color of the pond lit by the sun, illuminated now by the moon lowering behind me.

I hoped I had not made a mistake in touching her as her eyes filled with water and she began to cry.

I kept holding her as best I could, knowing what comfort we beavers felt from each other's touch, and reached back with my other paw, picking up one of the sticks and mimicking a grinding motion with my teeth before I handed it to her. She was smart and did what I showed her to do, biting down for relief.

Her tears slowed and I saw her concentration deepening as she squeezed her eyes shut and took a deep breath.

I brought the rest of the pile of sticks to her and again resumed my position by her side.

Before I knew it, the human kit came gliding out. It was a girl. I thought of Gigi then and how much joy this news would bring her. And of Penny and how much renewed respect I had for her after what I had seen there.

The kit was crying, and I knew she was hungry. And then Livia did what I'd seen Penny do dozens of times before as she taught the little ones to suck from her teats and quench their hunger.

Livia sighed as the liquid began to flow.

I saw the light of morning beginning to ascend in the east behind her. There was a glow from within her, too.

Before I left her, I said, "Congratulations. You are a mother now. You have a beautiful daughter. I do not know about her father, and I hope it is not presumptuous of me to propose this, but if you like, you can think of me as a kind of uncle to her. This is our pond, and we are happy to share it with you. As I said, we think of you as family. And that includes her. When she is ready, I will introduce my kits to her – and to you. You can be a kind of auntie to them, I think, as we make our way together. Every living thing knows that the world has changed, and it is harder to live on the earth now. So we can band together as sister and brother. You chose this pond, so we choose you and your daughter. We are family."

She smiled at me. I had no idea how much of what I'd said she could possibly understand. But it made me happy when she reached out her hand to me, patted my back, and said these words.

"Thank you. I will never forget what you've done for me."

Livia

I did not know that giving birth to another would mean giving birth to a new self, as well.

The next few nights were a different kind of labor for me than the one I'd spent riding the waves of pain that brought my girl into the world. Even when I wasn't awake at night to nurse her, I found myself sleepless and watching the world in a new way.

It was as if a night world opened itself to me, and in so doing, a night self emerged, too. These darker things were not scary, though, as I would have thought they would be. There was, I discovered, a kind of protection and depth of being that the darkness afforded me.

The first thing I pondered was what to name her. I thought about the nickname I'd given her, Beaver Girl, based on where we were, how the beaver pond had become our home and the beavers our friends and neighbors, as well as how she swam in the deep waters of me before her arrival. I pondered shortening this to B.G., and that made me think of that old musical group that my mom and Katrina liked called the Bee Gees.

It made me almost laugh out loud to remember the way the two of them would sing, imitating that high falsetto on the vinyl records some Saturday nights after a little too much wine. They were silly and funny and nerdy in the best possible way, and these memories coming back to me in those first few nights after the birth were the first ones I'd had since they were gone that really, truly made me happy. Happy wasn't quite the word for it, though. Alive. Feeling. A love.

I tried to remember any of the songs on that album and sing them as a kind of inside joke to myself and lullaby to the baby, but I found that my mind was foggy from exhaustion – not only the lack of sleep I'd had since the birth, but all I'd been through, the stress and loss and overwhelm of it all. I found I couldn't remember the past very clearly anymore.

As hard as I tried, the only song I could remember were "How deep is your love?"

I didn't even know if that was the name of the song itself or just a line from it—and it didn't really matter because it was all I could remember anyway, and so I ended up singing it softly and repeatedly to myself as I rocked my little baby girl.

"How deep is your love? How deep is your love? How deep is your love?"

It started as a question, and then as I heard myself repeating it, the words transformed into a sentence. A statement.

"How deep is your love. How deep is your love. How deep is your love."

I sang it to her, and I sang it to myself. I sang it in memory of my mother and Katrina and their love for each other. I sang it to Mouse in celebration of our sisterhood. I sang it to the pond itself. To the world of night shadow and starlight and the moon's constantly changing face. To the round paleness of my breasts that were miraculously feeding my baby. To the round earth herself.

And in this way, it became a kind of praise song of awe and wonder to the world.

"How deep is your love! How deep is your love! How deep is your love!"

Sometimes I had to pause in my singing because my voice became choked with tears of amazement and joy.

This is what I meant when I said I became someone else. My former self would have been gripped by worry about how all of this could even be possible. She would have wanted plans and answers, a reassurance that there would be enough food to eat and that the shelter would protect us in the coming winter.

But becoming a mother washed so much of that away from me.

There was no way I could have planned to have a baby in the middle of a swamp while a beaver sat next to me and comforted me. It was impossible for me to know how much love would come pouring out of me after her birth. And added together, the existence of both events meant that I released the grip I'd had on what I thought was possible in life.

I think what happened to me out in the world again next to the beaver pond in the middle of the night is that I discovered faith.

It wasn't religion, and it wasn't even a god or goddess, exactly. It wasn't what humans had for centuries called faith, which struck me now as a kind of looking in the mirror and then sketching out a fantasy based on what qualities we wanted to emphasize in ourselves by projecting them onto a greater being.

This faith was not that. It was much bigger. And completely beyond me and what I'd known about myself as a human.

It was a kind of opening to something much greater. And a release of what I could control.

A deep knowing. And at the same time, an abandonment of ever really knowing anything completely.

I opened to love for my daughter and the world. And I let go of any desire to dominate her or it. I knew without a doubt that I was loved unconditionally by her and by the world itself. And I could never, in my limited, human way, know the immensity of the bigger picture or how all the pieces fit together.

It was about relationship.

Faith, I felt deep within me like a seed beginning to sprout, was knowing that I was in relation to my daughter in the same way that the world was in relation to me.

And that these were not things, not facts or abstract principles, as I'd been taught by biology or psychology or any of the other sciences or studies of what humans had called logical.

These were beings. Alive. Knowing. Feeling. A love. And I was part of it, too.

As the moon waned and lit the darkness less and less over the next several days, I pondered all these things that were not things, both in my heart and all around me.

And then it came to me. Like a sound almost, whispered across the water to me.

Beej. I remembered this word from when my mother meditated. She taught it to me one morning when I was very young, and I woke up before the sun came up and heard something. I walked from my bed – I must have only been a toddler then because I remembered it was a little bed, low to the ground, and in the house where we lived before we moved to a new house with Katrina and Mouse – and I made my way through the dark, following the sound of my mother's voice until I found her in the dark on the floor of her room.

She was sitting on a round cushion in front of a candle, and her eyes were closed, and she was singing something softly again and again.

When she heard the pitter patter of my steps in my little jumpsuit pajamas, she opened her eyes and smiled at me.

"Hey, little Liv," she said to me. "You're up early." She opened her arms to welcome me into her lap. She was warm and soft as she held me.

"What is that sound you're making, Mama?" I asked.

"It's called a beej mantra," she said. "The word means 'seed' in Hindi. That's a language that people speak in India, which is where yoga comes from."

"You're saying a seed?" I asked.

She laughed. "That's almost it," she explained. "It's like I'm planting a seed with my voice out loud in the world."

I pondered this then as a toddler – and when I remembered that moment later by the pond, it occurred to me that the seed of who I would become as a woman had been planted in the small girl I was when I sat in my mother's lap.

"Another meaning for beej is beginning," my mother said to me. "Everything begins as a seed. Even you. Even me." And she kissed my cheek, carried me back to bed, and rubbed my hair back from my forehead until I fell back asleep.

"Beej," I said to my daughter, kissing her on the cheek like my mother had with me. "You are the seed. You are the beginning."

And my daughter had her name.

Chap

Penny nursed the new litter of kits, as she always did, from the time the moon was whole and round like a pond in the sky until she hid her light and left the night world dark for three nights.

It was as if the moon planned it like that so that the first night the kits ventured out with us to begin to collect their own food from the pond, they would always be protected by the deep ink written by the moon's absence.

Of course, all six of them were scared, as each litter had been before them, which was only natural. The water way allows the arising of this wave of frightened feelings to keep us alert when we are doing something new for the first time. But Penny and I, along with their older siblings, encouraged them, and stayed close to them, and praised them as they made their way.

And there was so much new for them to do!

They had to crawl down into the main entrance hall of the lodge for the first time. As I'd seen each litter do before them, they slipped and slid a bit. We laughed with them then and told them that all creatures lose their footing when going in a different direction for the first time.

And when learning to swim, the moment before entering the water is always the scariest part for young kits.

What will happen? What if it doesn't work? What if you sink? What if you fail?

These thoughts keep us cautious so we don't take unnecessary risks, but at some point, we must abandon them and just jump in.

It was mostly a matter of trust.

Their buoyant little beaver bodies knew what to do. The blubber helped them float. Their tails acted as rudders to guide them in the direction they wanted to go. Their little back paws, webbed and spread behind them, kicked in unison and propelled them as they swam.

We laughed again, Penny and I, remembering this moment for our kits with each of our litters – when they discovered the real meaning of being a beaver.

Water.

They splashed and played. They chased each other. Hero and Happy rolled around and around each other like floating logs as they wrestled. Mick and Meadow floated on their backs as they gnawed on the sweet leaves of lilies. Gaia and Gem made water their playmate and friend.

Penny and I had taught each succession of kits that water was their friend.

And most years, it had been.

But not the year that our third litter came.

It started as rain.

We had already said goodbye to Midge and Chuck, our first two kits, and we were raising three more who were yearlings, and our third litter was already learning to float and paddle and eat on their own after weaning from their mother.

There were six newborns that year, too, so we had nine altogether in the pond that late summer night when it started to rain.

"Chap," Penny called to me on the other side of the nine kits as we kept watch over all of them. "It's coming down too hard."

She was right. She always was. And I'd learned enough from our years together to listen to her.

I nodded and responded.

"Let's get them in," I said.

They didn't want to go, of course. The yearlings knew enough to listen when their mother had that tone of alarm in her voice. But the newborns were just discovering the joys of being on their own in the water and complained when we cut their playtime short.

"Whack!" Penny slapped her tail against the water in warning to let them know that she was serious.

Deadly serious.

They swam reluctantly to the entrance of the lodge then.

We stayed inside for four nights and four very long and dark days. I'd never heard rain so loud. My mind almost didn't want to believe it was the same water that had provided me with my lodging and livelihood my whole life long. It felt as if it had turned into another element altogether. Hard as rocks. Burning as fire. Whipping as wind.

Penny and I huddled around the kits and tried to hush them. There was nothing we could do about the rain. We could imagine the destruction it was heaping upon the dams we'd constructed. We knew the water in our pond was rising just as it was in the entrance ways to the lodge.

From time to time, I ventured to the cache to bring back soggy twigs and limp greens for everyone to eat. But food was little consolation. We chewed in a disconsolate way.

The boredom and anxiety were reaching their pitch when the rain finally slowed. It was the middle of the day, but we were all awake. There was only so much sleeping we could do when we were used to working hard night after night and were forced to stay in one place.

At first, even the sun was afraid to show her face. She glowed behind dark clouds as I left the lodge to check on the condition of the pond.

The pond, though, was no pond. Water had risen in the land all around us, and we now lived in a lake.

How much worse it would have been had we not constructed dams all around us, I cannot say.

The trees we'd been working on only a few nights before were now all standing in water. The banks were far away. The landscape of our home had completely changed, I realized, as my family gathered around me to survey the damage.

"Oh, Chap," Penny sighed. I nuzzled against her and said nothing. Neither did she, I knew, for fear of worrying the kits further.

Water was always flowing downward, I knew. It was the nature of water. Rain came down. Water rolled down mountain streams. Rivers flowed to the sea.

The work of beavers was to keep all this motion in balance, to create places where water could slow and stand long enough to support the life that the world depended upon. Humans and animals and birds and reptiles and amphibians and fish, yes.

But insects, most of all. And insects were the protein food source that so much of the living world depended upon.

And on that afternoon, with the sun hiding her face, and my partner and kits seeing the devastation that water could make, I heard no insects.

Not a hum or a buzz or flutter. No vibration. Not a small whine or whirr. Nothing teeming in the pond that had flooded over its banks. No small wings to pulsate. No droning of bees or wasps or mosquitoes. No purring of dragonflies and damsel flies. The hubbub of the insect world had fallen silent.

It was the absence of the flapping and waving and quivering and trembling and flickering that scared me the most after the flood that day.

Eventually, we recovered. Penny and the kits and I restored the land to its former balance, and the yearlings left the next year, and the newborns eventually did, too.

But I never forgot the terror of water, and it made me more cautious as a father and partner.

Gaia was the first of the newborns to venture onto the land. She heard the cries coming from the baby human and was curious. She slipped a bit on the mud as she emerged from the water, and then she found her footing. I kept an eye on her and swam near her in the water, but I let her go on her own.

She walked slowly, pausing occasionally to stop and listen for predators, as we'd taught her that she'd have to do, until she was almost to the shelter. She hunkered down next to a cypress tree, almost hidden by one of the knees next to it. And listened.

"Beej," I heard Livia whisper to her daughter. "You have a friend coming to visit."

Livia tilted her arms so the baby's head was leaning in the direction of Gaia.

"Isn't she cute?" Livia cooed. "So little and so fluffy."

And then Livia's voice became a tad bit louder as she said to Gaia, "You're welcome to come as close as you feel comfortable. We promise never to hurt you."

Gaia was cautious, though, and stayed where she was. I saw her watch as the baby latched on to the woman's breast in the same way that the kits did with their own mother. I could almost hear Gaia's mind working to make the connection between beavers and humans then.

Maybe it was seeing the baby feeding that made her hungry because the next thing I heard was her back teeth grinding against her front and she picked up a twig from the ground and crawled back through the mud to return to the water to practice chewing her own meal.

Once Penny and I felt that all six of the kits had had enough exercise and enough to eat for the moment, we rounded them up to head back into the lodge. Henry, Gigi and Mack were a great help in this, for once little kits get a taste of the fun and sweetness of the water, it's hard to get them to stop.

But we had work to do, and the night was halfway over.

Penny stayed back in the lodge with the little ones while the yearlings returned to the pond with me, and we worked on some trees deeper in the forest, chipping away pieces to reinforce the dam in the north, taking advantage of the dark moon night to venture further away from the pond than I normally would with all three of them.

"I can't believe we were ever so little!" Mack said between bites of sweetgum.

"Oh, you were," I assured him. "All of you were," I added, not wanting to make him self-conscious that he was still smaller than Henry and Gigi.

"How long will it take them to be as big as we are?" Henry asked.

"About the same amount of time it took you," I chittered. "A full turn of the sun through the seasons. That is a year. That is why we call you yearlings."

"But what will we be then?" Gigi asked.

"A year from now, when the kits are yearlings, you will leave the lodge and venture out on your own to make your own home."

"What?" cried Mack. "I am certainly not ready for that!"

"You will be," I assured him. "Growth takes its time in the water way."

I looked around me at the trees, our brothers and sisters that provided us with food and shelter, in addition to giving us the ability to create our water world with dams, and I said, "You see the trees and how some of them are like the kits, small and just beginning to put out leaves. Others are like you, taller and sturdier, but still not yet ready for harvesting. But the tallest ones, they have been growing here for years and years."

"How many?" Henry asked.

I shook my head and gnawed a bit on the last piece of ash tree I'd been cutting before adding it to the pile beside me as I thought this over.

"Longer than your mother and I have been here," was my answer because I remembered that they were here when we'd first arrived.

"That's a long time!" gasped Gigi.

"Oh, I'm not that old!" I chortled. But I was not a young beaver anymore, and I knew it. Each year that went by, each litter we raised and let go into the world, I was getting older, too. And this made me rely more upon time itself.

I started sawing a new piece from the ash tree and thought about how the moon goes dark at just the time the new kits are ready to leave the lodge for the first time to learn to swim and eat on their own. I reflected upon the tilt of the sun that tells us when it's time to start hurrying to fill our cache with food for the winter. I even considered the way my body knew what time it was when I was sleeping so I could wake just before sunset and make my way around the perimeter of the pond to make sure it was safe for the rest of the family to join me.

It seemed to me then that there was a piece of time in everything in the world – the moon and sun, the trees, and even beavers.

I wondered about humans. I remembered the fire from a few weeks earlier that Livia had escaped and how this brought her to us. I thought about how she came here alone and how this probably meant that she lost her family. I winced to recall the destruction at the big dam that other humans had done. I trusted Livia – I'd watched her, first alone, and then with her baby, enough to know that she had a good heart and knew that we are all meant to be connected in the world like water.

But I worried about the other humans besides her.

And what they might do to my family and me. And to her and her baby. And to our home. To the trees and the water and the land and the air and to every living being who lived there.

Though I did not share these thoughts with my yearlings, it occurred to me that the problem with humans is that they'd forgotten what we had always known: that we were all part of the world, and that the world is alive. And our lives, too, depended upon the generosity of the world with us. And that we, in turn, depended upon our ability to share.

Livia

The first two weeks with Baby Beej went by like this, in a kind of daze, a haze of breastfeeding and sleepless nights and an overwhelming need to be awake to witness this newfound wonder for the world. I did my best to feed myself by fishing and gathering foods during the day so I could eat enough to feed my daughter who, it seemed, was like the beavers and most awake at night.

But as the moon waned and went dark, something within me turned to darker things, as well. Perhaps it was a simple lack of sleep that caused it. I might have been able to agree with this assessment if I'd still been in the other world.

I thought that world had disappeared. But on a completely moonless night, it returned like a ghost to haunt me.

I usually woke when Beej nudged me to nurse, but that night, I popped awake to find her slumbering peacefully beside me. My body, though, was on fire. It felt as if a storm had started in my veins. I could feel electricity zapping me. I wanted to flee.

I remembered feeling this way once before.

"Mom?" I said, quietly, at the doorway to her bedroom in the middle of the night.

She rolled over in the dark. "What is it, honey?"

"I'm not okay," I said, and burst into tears.

She sat up and lit the candle beside her bed.

"Come here," she said, patting the comforter next to her. Where Katrina used to sleep.

I could not speak at first. I was overwhelmed by all that had happened, the breakdown of the economy and the environment and everyone's health, and it felt as if something inside me was breaking, too.

She did not force me to talk. She just sat beside me, rubbing her hand softly across my back, and slightly nodding her head, as if my tears were words and she was listening carefully. And agreeing.

Finally, the deluge subsided, and I wiped my nose with the bottom of my t-shirt – the times of handing tissues to each other had long ago been over – and then I took a deep breath and said the thought that had woken me in the night.

"I don't think it's going to get better."

I saw her blue eyes widen in the circle of light from the candle as she looked at me, and at first, she opened her mouth to say something, but then her shoulders slumped down. She nodded and looked at her hands.

"Mom," I said. "You know it, too. I know you do. At first, you and Katrina kept things going, thinking ahead and making sure we had enough provisions to last for months. When other people started freaking out, you both allowed us to be calm. We felt ready. We felt it was like that storm that came that year. We just had to prepare, and get ready, and then ride it out."

A cloud came over her eyes as she blinked at me, remembering.

"But it wasn't just a storm, was it, Mom? It didn't last for a few days, and there was no government agency to come in and help us recover, was there? Not when Mouse got sick. Not when Katrina did. Not even when we heard the news about Oma in Germany. It wasn't just our country. The whole world was overwhelmed."

I knew it was hard for her to hear Katrina's name. I knew I was hurting her by saying these things. But I had no one else. So I kept going.

"Mom, I'm sorry," I continued. "But you're the only one I have. It's like I'm a little kid again, and it's just me and you against the world."

She smiled even though her tears were falling as we remembered singing that Helen Reddy song when I was little.

"The thing is, though, there isn't any world left either," I said.

There was nothing she could say to argue against what I was saying, and she knew it.

I started shaking. It was as if my body was an animal in pain and terror. It was beyond words. I had never felt anything like this before, and the depth of the fear in my body scared me even more than any thoughts my mind was making.

"Come on," my mom said, standing. "Get up."

I wasn't sure what she wanted me to do, but she was using her mom voice that meant no arguing or resistance would be tolerated, so I did as she said and stood up.

"Put on your shoes. Grab a jacket."

It was early fall and had just begun to get chilly at night. While I went to my room to do as I was had been instructed, I heard her putting on her shoes and getting her jacket from the hall closet.

"Let's go," she said, grabbing the keys from the ceramic bowl in the kitchen.

And we walked out the front door.

We went down our block toward the west – the same direction I'd taken on the morning when I'd left our house for the last time as the fires approached – without talking, just hearing the loud echoes of our shoes on the dark and quiet street in the middle of the night.

As we turned the corner at the end of the block, she said, "I used to do this when you were little."

"Do what?" I asked.

"Go walking in the middle of the night. There were times I would find myself so anxious that I couldn't sit still. I was shaking sometimes, just like you were in the bedroom. I hate that I know how you were feeling, but I do. And I found that when that happened to me, the only thing that helped was to strap you into a snuggly thing that kept you close against my body and start walking."

"I never knew that," I said quietly.

"It's not the kind of thing that you really want to share as a mother," she said.

"So why now?"

She didn't answer at first. We walked for almost a block more, and then she stopped and turned to me.

"Livia," she said slowly. "You will always be my daughter. But what you've been through – what we've both been through – it's changed us. We are not the same people we used to be. You must not rely on me in the way that you have in the past."

It hurt me to hear her say this, but I did not interrupt her.

"You must find ways to take care of yourself," she said firmly. "I will not always be here."

Then she turned and kept walking, and I hurried to catch up to her. She was the only person I had left in the world, and I wasn't about to lose her in the night.

Especially when I knew, deep down, that she was right.

I had been right when I woke in the middle of the night with the conviction that things would never get better.

And she had been right when she told me she would not always be with me.

That had been almost a year ago. And now, shaking in the night in the middle of the forest with my own baby daughter sleeping next to me, I felt that same quaking in my body as if I were the earth and tectonic plates were jarring against each other within me.

I tried to calm down. Breathe more deeply. I tried to relax each part of my body, but the muscles refused to let go. They had become as wooden as the trees surrounding me. The only thing I wanted was to get up and move. Like my mother before me.

I gathered some leaves and piled them close to the sleeping baby and stood up quietly. I felt my back moving from the horizontal position it had been in for many days and nights as I nursed her, and I sighed with relief at being vertical and upright. I stretched my arms above my head and heard the vertebra in my spine cracking. I bent over and let my arms dangle to the damp ground as my hips released their tension.

Standing up again, I decided I needed a break. My legs yearned to move. My mind was moving in circles as I grappled with the urge of wanting to leave my daughter and simply be alone in my body for a brief time. I walked slowly, taking one step at a time, and then looking back to see if she was still asleep.

At one point, I could not see her anymore and I was free.

Guilt swept through me, but my desire to breathe on my own compelled me to keep going. I circled around the pond once, and after losing my footing and almost falling, I continued, being careful to move to higher ground in the places where the bank was muddy and slippery. Then after checking on Beej one last time, I decided to go deeper into the forest toward the east.

Again, I tried at first to move slowly to avoid tripping over cypress roots or falling into indentations in the soil covered with fallen leaves where old trees used to be. But it felt so good to be moving that I let myself take a chance and I began to run.

My lungs burned as they had that morning back at the house when the fires encroached, but this time, it was a good feeling. A stretching and yearning for air and freedom.

My legs and feet tingled from the exertion after being still for so long. I got into a rhythm. I let my arms swing. I found myself smiling.

Until I didn't.

Suddenly I was on the ground, and I couldn't remember what happened. My mind told me that I had tripped. That was the only logical explanation for why I was lying on the forest floor in the middle of the night bleeding.

My knees were scraped and stung as they released blood where the skin had been peeled away. But my right hand was what really worried me. My thumb was bent back at a sickening angle, and the pain was bone deep. I tried to stand, using my left hand to balance me, but a sharp pain in my shoulder stopped me.

I felt a wave of nausea, and at the same time, I felt my breath and heartbeat quicken as adrenaline kicked in.

What had I been thinking? What an idiot I was! How far was I from the baby? And how was I going to manage to get back? I berated myself and started to cry from the pain that was increasing, both physically and emotionally.

I may have hit my head. I started hallucinating. The beaver that had helped me on the night of my labor and birthing came to me. And this time, when he spoke, I understood him. And he understood me.

It was not just that I was listening to his sounds and sensing the meaning. I actually knew what he was saying.

"Livia, what have you done?" he said to me.

"A terrible thing," I answered.

I did not mean the fall.

"Tell me," he said softly.

I looked down at my knees. I remembered bleeding like this in the past. I felt the pain rising from deep within me. It had to come out. I opened my mouth to let it. But I didn't know how.

"I do not know how to begin," I said.

"At the beginning," he said.

The beginning. That was the meaning of the name that I'd given my daughter. And as much love as I felt for her, the great wonder I had at the miracle of her – there was, indeed, a darker beginning to her.

I felt bile rise in my throat as the images came back to me. They were like flashes of light on that dark night. Like the lightning strikes within my body.

This is what had awoken me, I realized then. This is what had scared me awake and gave me the impulse to get away. This is what made me run, and take this unnecessary risk, and end up on the ground.

This great guilt.

This horrible thing that I'd done.

I did not know if I could find the words to say it.

Chap

I had seen something like this before.

Beavers, like all creatures, survive many injuries over the course of a lifetime – those that happen to them and those they see others survive. Or not.

The last time it happened was when Mack had the tree fall on him, and his tail had been bleeding like Livia's knees were just then. But what I'd learned again and again as a parent of nine litters of kits was that after an accident like this, it's best to keep them talking.

The body wants to shut down. The mind wants to sleep. But my job was to keep them awake to tell the story.

The story of what happened. The story of how they were feeling. And the stories that could rise to the surface like old logs on a pond when the mind and body were in great pain.

This, I knew, was what Livia was going through. And like with my kits, she needed me to be there to bear witness.

"Tell me," I whispered to her gently.

"I do not know how to begin," she said.

"At the beginning," I responded gently.

And she did.

"The name I gave my daughter," she began to say. "The word means seed and beginning. I gave this name to her because I wanted us to start over. Have a new beginning out here, away from the world as it was. Plant a seed in this world."

I nodded. I could imagine what it would take for a human to be so alone. It was why I had welcomed her into our community.

"But there is another meaning," she continued. "I mean, there was another beginning."

She stopped.

I moved closer to her and placed my paw against her arm as I had once before on the night when her daughter was born. If she were going to be the mother her daughter needed her to be, she would have to keep going with the story.

She took a deep breath and let it out. She held up her right hand and looked at it. The thumb was swollen. She winced as she looked at it. And then continued speaking.

"It was last winter," she said. "I went to get firewood. The electricity grid was down, and I had withstood the cold for as long as I could in the house, but as the winter grew deeper, it was as if the cold moved into the house and refused to leave. I couldn't take it any longer."

I patted her to assure her I was listening.

"I was about to chop down a tree," she said and then stopped and smiled at me. "That's funny. I never thought of that before – how that's when it happened. When I was getting ready to cut a tree."

"We are more alike than you know," I said softly. "Keep going."

"He came up from behind me. I did not see him coming. He put his knee into mine and I crumpled to the ground. I cut myself on the saw as I went down. It was this hand," she said, lifting the injured one again to show me.

"I do not remember details about what happened next. I know what happened. But it is not a story I can tell. It's not that I'm trying not to tell you. It's that I don't have the full story. I have feelings – the pain. Flashes – the way the pine tree above me waved green and blue in the light reflected by the lake. It comforted me."

I certainly knew the comfort that trees could be. More than comfort, actually. Sustenance. Shelter. Life.

"When it was over, he said something to me. Suddenly, I wasn't numb anymore. I was angry. I had never felt such rage. It was a wildfire in me. I tried to vomit it out, but it continued to burn in me."

It was this wildfire that had brought her to me. Not just the wildfire raging through the land that destroyed her home. This deeper wildfire that impelled her to live this far away from other humans. That's what she was telling me.

"He started to walk away, and I stood quietly. It felt so good to be upright again on my own two feet. Some kind of energy was surging within me. I bent down to pick up the saw. I knew what I was going to do even before I did it. It was like it had already happened."

I stayed very still as I listened.

"He had done things to me with that saw," she said. "He cut me. He said horrible things as he did. I was bleeding all over. But I did not feel it until then. It was then that the pain became a conflagration."

She was starting to scare me.

"I followed him. I do not know how I managed it, but I was able to walk silently behind him. It enraged me that no one else would be able to tell what he had just done by looking at him. I wanted to mark him somehow. I wanted the world to know what he'd done."

Revenge. That's what made us different from the humans.

"At one point, he stopped to unzip his pants and pee against a tree. I knew I had my chance. I took the saw into both of my hands. I gathered all my strength into my shoulders and arms and lifted it above me. And then I brought it down into the side of his face."

I was frozen as she told me this. I had been expecting a different kind of story. A story of her pain. Not this. Not this violence. Not this same story of humans.

"He wheeled around toward me, but I had already brought the saw up again, and this time, I had a clear path into the front of his neck. And I took it."

I wanted to run away. But I stayed.

"I chopped him down. I cut him like he had cut me. Like I had intended to do with the tree before he stopped me. Repeatedly. I kept going. Even when he was down on the ground. Even when he was no longer breathing."

I was barely breathing, too.

"It's so weird," she said. "I remember all this so clearly, even when I can't remember much of what he did to me. But I can see his body, his bloody face and his neck, the way it spurted out in rhythm with his heartbeat. Until it didn't. I stood there looking at him on the ground when I was done. It was like I was memorizing it. I wasn't afraid. I didn't feel guilty. I was glad. Glad for what I had done. I felt that I had saved other women from being his victims like I had been. I was proud of myself, actually. Elated."

Now I really wanted to get away. I could feel my limbs twitching and the churning in my belly that were my body's way of signaling that it was time to flee.

"And that's the story of the beginning of my daughter's life. It wasn't long before I realized that she was coming. By then, I'd stopped leaving the house except at night to scrounge for food under the cover of darkness. I didn't want to see anyone else. The world was no longer a safe place. And I was part of it. It was in me, too—the destruction that had swept through. The virus, the gangs, the economic collapse, the constant storms, and crises in nature. The violence. It was in me, too."

I swallowed. My mouth was dry. I saw the beginnings of morning light in the sky. It was time for me to go. I needed to get back home to my lodge.

"I am not asking you to understand," she said quietly. "You were the one who asked me for the story. And now you have it. Thank you for listening."

I saw tears coming from her eyes. They were not from the pain of her fall.

I nodded and said, "This is a terrible thing you have been through. I am so sorry for your pain."

She placed her face into her hands, sobbing.

And I left her there. There was nothing more I could do. The light was turning yellow already between the trees on the eastern horizon. My family needed me. I needed to be safe.

As I made my way back to the lodge, I tried not to think about what she'd told me. But it would not leave me. A sense of grief and deep disappointment rose within me. I had considered her part of our family. But now I did not know if that was even possible. Maybe the human and animal worlds were simply too different. Maybe we could not trust her after all. I would have to find a way to discuss this with Penny, I decided. It was too much for me to hold all on my own.

And I worried for the baby. I was not sure how Livia could care for her with her injuries. Or how she would even manage to make her way back to the pond.

The pond. When I saw it, there was such relief that I dove straight in. I berated myself later that I did not even stop to check on the baby. I torpedoed directly to the entrance of the lodge. I was hungry but so exhausted that I had no energy to grab something from the cache.

After I dried myself off, I lay down next to Penny. I could not even look at her. I kept my eyes closed.

"What happened?" she asked.

I shook my head. I could not speak. I would tell her later, but right then, I needed to sleep. I needed to give my mind a break from what I had just heard. It was something that I had known all my life, but never had my body felt it as deeply as it did now.

Humans could not be trusted.

Livia

Chap left me as the sun came up, and for the first morning in as long as I could remember, I watched the sunrise with a sense of relief.

Not with the feeling that I could be seen. Not with the fear that someone would break into the house. Or find me on a street. Or hurt me.

In telling him what I had done, I had become clean.

Even though I was alone and still hurting, lying on the forest floor with a sore shoulder, bloody knees, and bent and swollen thumb, in addition to being hazy from a night without sleep and worried about needing to get back to my baby, it was as if I had finally washed away months of grime and mud that had been covering me.

I saw everything more clearly. Especially me.

The sunrise pierced through the cypress trees and created long shadows of line and light. Even these were sharper. The world was reflecting my inner being to me in vibrant stripes of wrong and right.

I felt my chest expand as I took a deeper breath and said out loud, "I didn't do anything wrong."

What I meant was this: before I told my story out loud, it had tipped the balance of justice with a heaviness that weighed my whole being down. I was not able to feel the feelings about what had happened to me because the grip of what I had done was trying to bury me.

The truth is that I would not have done what I did if he had not done what he did to me.

Cause and effect. Action and reaction. A body in motion stays in motion. These were the laws of nature that science had taught me. And there was no reason why this shouldn't also apply to me. I was part of nature, too. I had learned this out there in the swampy forest with the beavers and my baby.

For some reason then, I thought of a short story we'd read in school at the end of my junior year just before the summer when the virus came. It was called "A Jury of Her Peers," and it was about a lady who went missing and her neighbor and the sheriff who tried to figure out what happened. They walked through her house to get clues: her kitchen was a mess, the stitches on her sewing were uneven, and her pet bird was dead.

We didn't learn what she did exactly, but it was clear what had been done to her.

I'd read the story as a simple morality tale when I was 17. Now, only two years later, it took on a whole other meaning to me.

I was that lady.

And I had no jury and no peers of my own. But I did have one thing: I had told my story.

I had said what I needed to say out loud, and the world listened. The moonless night, the beaver beside me, the land who met my body when I fell and gave me a place to sit where I could tell it. These trees surrounding me now, in bright gold morning light, the sun itself who had been attending in the dark, waiting for his entrance.

These were the jury of my peers.

And they declared me not guilty.

And let me free.

I looked down at my knees, still bloody, but already the scrapes were beginning to heal. Katrina had taught me how healing happens. First, white blood cells rushed in to assess the situation. They were kind of like the first responders used to be. I may have forgotten all the details of the process, but I did recall the word microphages, which were like the old Pac Man game my mom used to play as a teenager that ate up all the damaged cells in the wound. And then the lymph system kicked in. They were the garbage men of the area that cleaned everything up by hauling it away.

All this activity, I knew, was already happening in my body right then without my conscious understanding. It knew what to do and it did it. It was happening, too, not just in the places that were bloody and scraped, but also in my thumb and shoulder where injuries had happened in my muscles and joints.

The pain meant something was happening, almost like a sacred ceremony, and all I needed to do was to rest, take it easy, and let it be.

The pain was part of the healing.

I heard her long before I could get to her. The sun was high behind my shoulders, and my body made a crooked shadow as I hobbled back to the pond. I felt the soreness in my shoulder, and it made my gait uneven. I held my thumb above the level of my heart to keep the pain and swelling from getting too bad. I walked like this as quickly as I could to get back to my baby girl, but her cries pierced through the woods and reached me long before I saw her.

My breasts were leaking milk by the time I entered the shelter. Her face was beet red, and her wailing was rhythmic, like a siren, not the soft cooing I'd heard her doing before when she was hungry.

I'd scared her by leaving.

I sat down as gently as I could, squatting slowly but not putting any weight on either arm. Then I lifted her quickly, despite the knives of pain I felt in my arms. My injured right hand turned away from her instinctively. As if my hand knew what it could handle without my brain even registering the thought.

I pulled up my t-shirt with my left hand as I cradled her in the crook of my right arm, and it was a moment before she noticed me again and could calm enough to drink.

But when she did, when she latched on and I could feel and hear her desperate gulping, we both sighed with relief.

"I'm sorry," I whispered to her. "I am not a perfect mommy."

She stopped drinking and leaned her head back and blinked her hazel eyes at me, and it was as if I were looking in a mirror.

"I know what it's like," I told her. "To have a mom who is the only person in the world for you. I knew what it was like when I was your age, and then for a long time, I had a real family."

I stopped. It had been so long since I said their names out loud.

"Mouse was my best friend," I said to Beej, as her drinking slowed, and I could see her belly puffing out contentedly. "She was so smart and funny. She was more than my best friend. She was my sister. When you get older, I will tell you stories about her."

I could see that she was full now, as her eyelids grew heavier, and the swallowing stopped.

"Her mother's name was Katrina. She was smart like Mouse, but tough, too. Strong. She took care of my mom and me. I will tell you more about her as you grow, too."

Beej was sleeping but I kept talking.

"My mom's name was Isabelle. She was beautiful and kind. She had eyes so blue it was like the sky was in them. Oh, she would have loved to meet you."

I paused. My chest ached with grief, and I let myself cry as I held Beej. I realized that the anger and the fear I'd been clinging to all these months that had allowed me to keep moving, keep going, simply survive, had also kept me from feeling any sadness.

"Mom," I said out loud. "I miss you so much. Can you see her? My baby daughter? I hope you can."

I looked out over the water on the pond and felt a slight breeze cross from west to east, rippling the surface and touching us gently when it arrived at our shelter.

"I am not perfect," I said to Beej, transferring her to my left arm despite the pain to give my right hand a bit of a break. "I won't promise you that I will be. But I will love you unconditionally and I will do everything in my power to take care of you and provide for you and keep you safe."

I felt as if she were listening because her little rose-shaped lips curled into a smile. I knew enough to know that babies don't really smile at that age and that it was probably just gas, but it made me happy anyway.

"But there's something else I want to promise you," I continued. "I know that a mom and daughter can be very close, and while this is special, there is such a thing as being too close if there is no one else."

I was admitting this to myself for the first time as I said it because, I realized, that my mom had been taken from me at the age when most girls are rebelling from their mothers to be able to forge their own identities. I hadn't had that chance.

"What I'm trying to say is that it won't just be you and me against the world. I have decided to stay here – I built this shelter for us here—because, as crazy as this might be, the beavers, I think, will be part of our family. They've been good to me. I think they will be good to you, too."

I was suddenly very tired as the sun headed toward the center of the pond. Beej snored softly and I heard it as a kind of lullaby and placed her gently on the ground in the shelter next to me.

"Beaver Girl," I whispered to her as she slept, almost asleep myself. "What I'm trying to say is that I can't raise you all by myself. And I don't know if there are any people left in the world that I can trust. So you will have to trust me when I say that our family is right here. In the trees. The water. The birds. The beavers. The bullfrogs. The wind."

I do not know if I actually said those words or simply dreamt them – so deeply did I sleep then – with my Beaver Girl snuggled next to me and the breeze from the west caressing me. I had done what I had to do in the night, walking like my mother before me. I had fallen and hurt myself, but still I had told my story. And I had returned to my baby. Despite the pain from my injuries, I had returned safely. And I was stronger now. And free.

Chap

A pink beam of dawn light came down through the air hole in the top of the lodge early the next morning as our kits slept, all nine of them, curled up together in the safety of our lodge.

Penny and I huddled near the entrance and whispered.

"I smell blood on you," she said.

It was true. I watched her little snout as she tried to discern where I'd been, and I knew that our sense of smell was that acute. It was how we survived – by avoiding the smell of humans.

"Human blood," she declared. "Chap, what happened?"

I made a low rumble, not wanting to go over it again, but I knew I had to. She was my partner for life. She was the one I trusted, even with my own life. And I'd depended upon her during all the years we'd raised kits together. I knew she deserved to know what I now knew about our human neighbor at the pond.

"I was out in the eastern forest last night," I began. "I found a stand of poplars for us to process to add to our cache this fall, and I was assessing what would need to be cleared to make a path so all the kits could work together to drag the sticks back to the pond more easily."

She nodded. This was something we'd done many times before. We didn't want to harvest the trees too near the pond so heavily that the younger kits couldn't learn the skills they'd need to survive on their own when they were older.

"And then I heard something. At first, I froze. It was dark. There was no moon. But gradually, I saw that it was Livia. She had fallen and was hurt."

Penny crooned softly in sympathy.

"So I went over to her to see what I could do for her. I had come to consider her as a member of our family."

Penny's eyes narrowed, taking in the past tense of my statement.

"Had?" she asked.

"Well, what happened next is that she told me something. A story I wish I did not know, honestly."

She turned toward me and put one paw on me, just as I'd done with Livia on the night when she gave birth to the baby.

"You remember we had wondered who the father of her baby was and what had happened to him," I continued. "I found that out last night. He was…" I hesitated and looked over at the kits.

"Violent with her," I whispered.

Penny growled softly from deep within her throat and belly, a protective instinct.

I nodded.

We sat quietly for a moment, thinking about the implications of this. For Livia and her baby. For us.

"Do you think he could return?" Penny asked finally.

I shook my head. "Definitely not."

Penny's eyes widened and she stayed very still as she listened to what I said next.

"She followed him. After. And she processed him like wood. She cut him. She was out trying to gather wood for her fire, and she had a sharp tool. He had used it on her to hurt her, and she used it on him in return. She did

172

not hold back. She ground him down. He did not give himself willingly like the trees. She took a life by force. She murdered him."

I heard Penny grinding her back teeth, considering what I had just said.

"I do not know that she can be trusted," I continued. "It scared me – her story. It brought up for me the long history of the cruelty of humanity. We can see what they've done to each other and to the land and air and water. What they did to our ancestors in the past. How they almost completely wiped us out. They clearly do not appreciate how we work so hard to keep it all in balance. Harmony."

She nodded but did not yet speak.

"What can we do, Penny? Should we move to get away from her? Would we be safer then?" I asked.

She stretched and glanced at our kits again before answering.

"The kits are the most important thing," she said. "They are too young for us to move just now, when they've only just begun to swim and eat on their own. And there's the human kit, too. She is, as you've said, a member of the pond family now. We must do what's best for her, too. If we move and abandon this pond, stop reinforcing the dams, the water will drain away eventually and the source of fresh drinking water and fish for food for the mother will disappear. That's not fair to that baby."

I hadn't thought of that. I was only feeling fear.

"Chap," she cooed gently. "If we abandoned them, we would be acting like the humans who do not understand the water way."

I nodded. She was right. The water way taught that everything is connected, and that as much as humans think they are separate from each other and the world around them, they are not.

"I understand that what she told you was upsetting," Penny said. "It is never easy to hear about the ending of a life. But we cannot let our reaction lead to another reaction. This is the way of humans, back and forth, injury after injury, and never leaving time for healing to begin."

I took a deep breath and exhaled, filled again with a sense of love for her, her wisdom, the gift she gave me as my partner for life.

"We won't leave," she said. "And we won't abandon them. We are beavers and we follow the water way. We know that everything is connected. We know that life does not exist without water. We work hard, night after night, to keep the water clear and clean. We do the work that everything else in the world depends upon us to do. We always have. And we always will."

She nuzzled my neck and kissed me. We snuggled together after moving closer to the kits. I felt her breath slowing as she lay down next to me, soft and warm. She was such a comfort to me. And so much more. She was the real leader of our family.

And that included Livia and Beej. Penny's decision that we would stay had taken the lives of others, their well-being, into consideration, as well as ours. That was the way of the beaver. We did not do all the work we did night after night just for us alone. We did it for the fish and the dragonflies and garter snakes and wood frogs and green frogs and red efts and painted turtles and herons and egrets and otters and mink and muskrats. And humans, too.

I sniffed and could smell Livia returning even before I heard her. Her steps, slow and uneven, as her body with its injuries made its way back to her shelter. And her baby.

I heard Beej screaming like our kits sometimes did at that stage when they were overly hungry, persistent wailing noises to entice the mother closer so she would feed them at once.

I heard Livia settling into the shelter and then the rustle of leaves as she picked up Beej and brought her to her body.

The deep sigh of the baby and the first swallows of milk, long and deep, after a night without her mother. A soft cough when she caught her breath and the eventual slowing of their heartbeats in synchrony together as the nearness of each other fed them in more ways than just physically.

Their sighs in unison. They were united and peaceful once again. I closed my eyes and silently spoke to them in my mind.

"We are all together again. As a family. You are part of this pond and this land and this water and this air that we all breathe together. Penny helped me to remember that today, and I will not forget it again. I promise to work as hard as I can to take care of the dams and the canals and the ponds that all life depends upon. I do this for both of you, and I do it for Penny and the kits, and for all beings who rely upon all the work that I do. This is my solemn pledge to you."

Livia

The night after I'd fallen in the forest, I slept so long and so deeply that I woke the next morning feeling a tide of strength rising within me. It was as if the pain of my recent injuries – and the older pains I'd held within me – had finally receded from the shore of my body.

I had survived.

I was no longer a victim. Yes, my best friend had died, and after that, her grandmother. And then her mother. And my mother was gone, too. But these were not losses that had happened *to* me.

How could they be? I was not the center of the universe. The pond had taught me that. I breathed the fine air and drank the clean water and ate the fresh fish that the pond made possible. I had not created these things. They were gifts to me.

The deaths, the losses I'd suffered, I realized that morning, were not mine alone. They were part of something larger.

Did I feel anger? Certainly. Were the deaths unnecessary, caused by a lack of leadership and denial of accountability? Definitely. But to stay in the cycle of anger and blame and revenge was not healthy. It did nothing to help me recover.

It would not help me be a better mother.

As I looked down at my daughter's little round face, her cheeks working to drink the milk flowing from me, I knew that one day, she would face death, too.

I was not afraid of this realization. It seemed to me, in that moment, a kind of revelation. A beautiful thing.

That each mother on earth – not just human, but beaver and bird and turtle and fish and every insect, too – gives birth to the next generation with the knowledge that death will come eventually to the offspring, so tiny and new.

It is the pact we make with the larger pattern of what I was coming to call faith.

Destruction, like the three nights of darkness that the moon went through each month, was simply part of the cycle.

I had not been able to hold funerals for the members of my family who died, but that morning beside the pond, I felt somehow that the birds singing their praise songs to the morning light were helping me to honor and remember my family in a good way for the first time.

It had been the release that telling my story had given me that brought me into this place of understanding. Humility. Gratitude.

I would not take anything back, I realized, bringing Beej up to my shoulder to pat her back once she'd had enough to drink, because everything that happened led to this moment, and to her life with me right then.

Looking out over the pond, I noticed ripples intersecting near the lodge and several small brown heads bobbing up above the surface of the water.

The kits were coming closer!

Beej had a nice, deep burp, and then I turned her so she could face our friends as they swam nearer to us.

They did not come directly onto the land as the little one had done before but waded near the shore and paddled in place. I tried to count them all but there were so many, and they kept moving in and out, up and down, in the water in front of me.

And then a large one approached me. It was not Chap, not the one who'd been with me the night Beej was born or the night before when I had fallen. I saw the sagging belly and distended teats and realized this must be the mother of the new babies.

177

She walked slowly on all fours for a few steps and then rose up on her hind legs as I'd seen Chap often do. She held her paws in front of her and rested them on her belly.

She was a slightly lighter color than Chap. Her copper eyes had touches of light in them from the morning sun behind me as their round shape caught the yellow reflections. Her snout was rounder than Chap's, too, and her cheeks were chubbier.

I smiled at her. "I'm Livia," I said. "This is my daughter, Beej."

She nodded and whistled back to her kits, and as I watched them, I remembered the words from a book my mother had read to me about puppies when I was little: roly poly, tumble bumble, pell mell they came onto the shore.

Six of them!

They stayed behind her, trying to stay shielded by her body and at the same time curious about me.

"I'm Penny," she murmured softly. "And these are my new kits."

As she said each name, they stepped forward and bowed slightly. I could not believe this was happening, but I was learning to let go of my expectations for what was possible in the world.

"Happy," she said, and he blinked at me, and I swear it looked like he smiled. I smiled back.

"Gaia," she called, and I recognized her from our earlier encounter. I smiled at her, too.

"Mick," she said next, and the littlest one bowed his head shyly. I did the same to show him he had nothing to fear from me.

"Gem," was her next kit, and I noticed the beautiful brightness of her fur, almost cinnamon and gold in the morning light.

178

"Hero," she said, and I sensed pride in her voice when the largest male came forward. He had a stripe on his back unlike the others.

"And Meadow," she called to the last one, who'd become distracted and wandered back to the shore before returning to her mother when she heard her name.

"We are so happy to meet you all!" I said, grinning wildly, shaking my head in wonder. "Aren't we, Beej?" I cooed, bouncing her up and down gently on my lap as she gurgled and made bubbles with her tiny mouth.

Penny whistled again, and all the kits dove directly back into the pond in unison. I was amazed at how quickly they seemed to disappear as the ripples faded and I couldn't even tell that they'd been there only a moment before.

"I want you to know I consider you a sister," Penny said to me. "You are part of our family, and I welcome you and your baby and vow to you to treat you as a member of our family and I expect you will do the same for me. For us."

I nodded slowly. "I promise," I said solemnly. "I am honored to be included."

"Good," she said, and I could see the muscles in her back relaxing slightly. "Well, it's bedtime for us, so I must get back to the lodge and settle my kits down for the night. Chap is still out with our three yearlings. They went to work on the big dam overnight but should be back shortly. It was nice to meet you, Livia. And little Beej, too."

"Nice to meet you," I said, barely able to get the words out, overcome by the marvel of what was happening.

Not long after the V of ripples that the water traced as she swam back to the lodge had faded away, I saw more brown figures swimming into the pond from the southern waterway. Chap and his three yearlings were returning from the big dam as Penny said they would.

But as I looked more closely, I saw that I was wrong.

Chap

Because the big dam was the farthest distance we had to travel for upkeep, I decided to take all three yearlings with me on the second night of the dark moon. The cover of darkness, I thought, would work to keep us all safer.

The night started out as it always did, as I woke before sunset and swam the perimeter of the pond to check for predators, and then we all gathered in the pond to have our first meal after sunset. We decided that Penny was going to stay close by the lodge with the kits who day by day were growing by leaps and bounds and yet still needed to keep learning how to gather their own food and be independent. They would be with us for two more years, I knew, because there was so much we had to teach them, but with each litter of kits that we had, it seemed those first days of their tiny cuteness went by more and more quickly.

All of us chose our own breakfast. I chewed on a bit of willow to relax my muscles that were still stiff from after the stress I'd encountered the night before. Henry munched on some of the poplar he'd been working on previously, gradually whittling away at the trunk that was as wide as his body was long. Gigi gnawed on a soggy branch of the cedar she'd completed that had fallen away into the pond. And Mack, as always, preferred to roll in the water with the lilies, which were sweeter than trees and took less work to harvest.

Once I felt halfway full, I whistled to let the three of them know it was time to go. It's best not to start out working with completely filled bellies. I'd found it takes away from the alertness we would need to complete the task.

We glided through the canals quickly in the dark, our bodies soundlessly swimming just beneath the surface of the water. I was proud of my family as I paddled behind them and watched the strength of their almost fully grown bodies.

All three of them knew the way by now, and I saw how skilled they were at moving over the smaller dams we had built along the way, not stopping to chat as they had when they were younger and far less disciplined. They knew the land was where we were most vulnerable and restrained themselves to keep the whole family safe.

Finally, we approached the big dam and dived low into that pond to inspect the foundation. The rocks that Henry and I had moved into place a few weeks before were still holding, but there were a few places where the heavier tides from the full moon and the rains that came after had created leaks between them.

I used my hind lips to keep water out of my throat and told Henry to get to work on those repairs. He was the strongest of the three of them, and I knew he would have the strength to make the long dives it would take to put the new sticks and mud into place carefully.

Then I headed to the surface with Mack and Gigi to check the top of the dam. I went first, popping my head above the water while they waited below for me to see if it was safe.

Once I gave the signal, they joined me, and we floated on the surface to examine the walls and top surface. Not much needed to be done, actually. I was proud of the quality of our construction.

But there were some reinforcements we could make to prepare for the rising of the waters in the coming weeks as the moon's light came back again. I showed Mack where I knew there was a good hickory stand, which was the strongest wood in the forest, and told him to go harvest long strips to place on the surface.

Gigi and I started by gathering mud in our paws to plug the smaller places where water was bubbling through. She worked in a calm and steady manner that reminded me of her mother.

I could see Henry as he popped up occasionally from being down below and headed straight to the shore to gather more of the materials he needed. But Mack was too far from me. I could not see him. I heard the grinding of his teeth against the hickory, though, and I knew he was doing his duty.

Time passed, and then an owl called, and the crickets paused to listen. In the silence of that intermission from the steady song of night, I heard something that was not right.

Clang!

Nothing in nature rang out like that – with a sharp sound and the echoing reverberation of metal against metal.

I swiveled in the direction of the sound – Mack!

I heard him call out for my help, and I zoomed directly through the water and onto the bank to run to him as fast as I could.

When I arrived, it was just as I had feared – his leg was caught in a cold and rusted metal trap set by humans.

He cried and whimpered, and as gently as I could, I admonished him to stay quiet. The humans could still be near, and we didn't want to attract their attention. He did as I told him to do, but his eyes revealed the great pain he was in as tears fell silently down the soft furry slope of his face.

This had only happened once before in my lifetime. And that time had been even worse. That trap had been a deadly one that caught one of my yearlings in its jaws, right over her back, and there had been no way to save her. I winced at the memory of the blood all over her.

This trap, though, was meant to catch a beaver without killing him.

But there was no way to escape without losing the leg.

I took a deep breath and told Mack the truth.

"I will, or you will—one of us will," I began. "We have to bite you out of this trap if you want to be let go."

His eyes grew wide and bright with terror.

"It's the only way, son," I said, as gently as I could. "Otherwise, you will stay here. And the humans who set this trap will return. They will take you away."

I could see his mind working to try to find another solution to the conundrum. There was none.

"Of course, it's your decision," I told him. "You are old enough to decide for yourself what you want to do."

He looked at me with such grief, and then he looked down at his leg in the trap. I remembered the day the tree had fallen on his tail, and I believed he was remembering that pain, too. He bent down and touched his leg with his snout, trying to figure it out.

Then he looked back at me.

"I can't do it, Papa," he said mournfully. "I'm sorry."

I stayed very still as I took in what this meant. What it would mean for him, and for our whole family. Especially Penny.

I bowed my head. It was not an acceptance I was giving him, exactly, but a kind of respect I knew parents had to grant their grown children eventually. To let them make their own decisions. No matter the consequence or pain.

"Okay, son," I said. "I understand."

Then I went to do what I had to do next: I went back to the dam and called to Henry and Gigi to come so we could say goodbye.

I had no words to tell them, so I simply led them back to the hickory stand and let them see with their own eyes what had happened to Mack.

"Papa!" Gigi cried. "There has to be a way to free him!"

I saw in Henry's eyes he knew what that way would be. And that his little brother would never choose that solution.

"We must respect Mack's decision," I told Gigi. "It is his life. His body. He must be the one to choose."

Gigi was crying as she nuzzled up to her brother and said, "I love you so much. I am so, so sorry."

Henry walked over, too, and Mack leaned against him, as he always had with his larger brother. They both allowed themselves to cry but they exchanged no words. The feelings they were having were too deep for any sound to express meaningfully.

I swallowed hard, steeling myself for what came next.

The light was rising on the horizon.

"Mack," I said to him in a voice as strong and calm as I could make it. "I am proud of you. Your mother and I love you. Always. You are a good son, and you will survive this. I know you will."

Tears of relief flooded his eyes as he registered that I respected his decision.

"But the sun is rising, and we have to return to the lodge now," I said.

He nodded.

Reluctantly, we all kissed him one more time and told him we loved him once again, and then we headed back home.

And left him on his own.

Livia

There are no words for what I heard next.

To call it a shriek or scream, squeal or screech does not do justice to the wrenching heartbreak of the sound. It was Penny, I found out later, who was mourning the loss of her son Mack at the hands of a trapper.

Man.

Chap came to tell me soon after. Even though the sun was bright overhead, and the pond was not a safe place for beavers in full daylight, he took a chance and swam to me as I sat with Beej on the bank wondering what had happened and why only two of the yearlings had returned with him in the morning light.

"Let me help," I said, standing up directly. "Maybe there's something I can do."

I was not afraid. I was enraged. And I hoped it was not too late.

"But the baby," he said to me. "You can't take her. It's too risky. There will be humans nearby who will come to check the trap."

I had held Beej for so long, night and day, that she was a part of me. I looked at her now, in my arms, and I knew he was right. I had already fallen once and was still sore and bruised from that night. How much help could I be in freeing Mack from a trap with a baby in my arms?

But what could I do?

"I can watch her," Chap said.

I cocked my head.

"How?"

"I'll stay with her. I will defend her with my own life," he said. "We do not like to do it, but when beavers have occasion to defend ourselves, we can rise to it quite easily. These teeth that cut wood can cut a man down swiftly."

I froze in my spot, remembering what he knew about me. We were alike in this way, he was telling me. Our ability to defend ourselves and those we loved.

"Okay," I said slowly, looking around. "Where should I put her?"

"Your shelter is best, I think," he said. "Against the back wall. That way she will be shaded, and I can sit in front of her."

I took a deep breath. I did not have much time to ponder. Mack was out there. At least, I hoped he still was.

I gave Beej a kiss and placed her in the shelter. I patted Chap on the back.

"Thank you," I said.

"And thank you," he responded. "Do not worry. I will guard your daughter for you."

"And I will do my best to find your son."

With that, I turned around and headed down the south bank of the pond toward the stream in the direction of the river where Chap had told me I would find the big dam and Mack in a trap near a hickory stand.

I wanted to run, but my knees were still sore from two nights before, and I didn't want to risk another fall, so I walked as quickly as I could, keeping my eyes down for roots and rocks and holes and indentations. The ground is never smooth in the forest even when it is flat.

I made my way swiftly, and although I had no clock, I guessed it took me almost an hour to arrive at the dam at my pace. I estimated that I was several miles away from our pond. I thought about how long this might have taken the beavers at night if they'd had to move only over land, and I could see the wisdom of the canals and creeks that helped them travel more easily even as they contributed to the upkeep of the watershed.

The dam was a grand engineering feat. It stretched probably thirty feet across the waterway, and although I could not see how deep the water was, I could tell that it held back a mighty flow that led to the river and created a large pond there. I would go so far as to call it a lake, and even at midday, it was filled with herons and egrets along the banks, sitting up in the trees in the sun, conversing quietly, and then landing near the shore for fishing from time to time. It was quite a beautiful sight.

But I had no time to waste. I headed north of the dam to where Chap had told me I would find the hickories. I knew they were trees with nuts, but it was still summer and too early for the trees to produce their harvest, so I had to guess at what I wanted to see.

The edge of the water was mostly willow and river birch, so I walked further back. I found myself stopping and listening as I'd seen the beavers do – in case I could hear Mack or those who had set the trap for him.

Soon I came upon a stand of large trees, almost as tall as the ash, which were they tallest in the forest with upper branches that looked like umbrellas that had been folded up backwards in a storm. These trees had wider trunks, though, and were the gray color of some oaks, but shaggier, as if the bark was tangled hair that had not been brushed in a long time.

I stopped again, listening.

I wasn't sure at first, but I thought I heard a soft nasalized greeting. It sounded like the summer wind whispering through the long, pointy leaves of the trees that rustled almost like palm fronds. But it was not coming from above. I looked around me at the forest floor.

There, near the base of a large hickory, was Mack, his left front leg caught in a metal ring.

"Mack!" I cried, ignoring my wounded knees as I knelt to him.

He looked at me with eyes so round and brown that they reminded me of the profound feeling I'd had once while watching a lunar eclipse with my family when I was in middle school. We'd woken in the middle of the night and set up chairs in the front yard to be able to have a good view as the moon turned pink and then red and then completely dark.

I examined the metal ring. It was attached to two metal posts that led to a larger, rectangular piece that I guessed was the spring, and on the other side of that was a chain leading to a piece that staked the contraption into the ground so he could not get away.

His leg was bloody, and I was not sure if this was because he'd tried to free himself or simply from the violence of the sharp metal when he'd been caught.

"Oh, poor baby," I cooed to him. "It's okay. I'll help you."

I fiddled with the rectangular piece, trying to figure out how to unlatch it. There must be a way to do it, I figured, without hurting him further, as I knew beavers had been trapped almost to extinction for their pelts to make fashionable felt hats in the early centuries of white expansion in North America.

I looked for a piece that would slide back and forth. I ran my fingers along the top and bottom of the rectangle until I felt a latch. Even though the spring had already gone off to catch Mack's foot, I was still cautious as I felt for the direction that would unfasten the lock.

I heard a pop, and at the same time as the latch swung back, the trap opened, and Mack was free.

He did not move at first. I thought it might be because his foot hurt him, but then I saw a figure behind me reflected in his eyes.
Man.

I wheeled around to see him standing behind us, and in his hands, he held a long pole with a net at the end.

"Run!" I yelled to Mack as I stood up to face the man and shield Mack from him.

I did not look back but heard leaves rustling and then the soothing splash that meant he'd made it into the water and could head swiftly and safely back home.

Whether I could do the same, though, was another matter.

Chap

Beej stared at me with the same pondwater-colored eyes that her mother had as I sat beside her to protect her.

I sniffed after Livia for as long as I could, and when I lost the scent, I knew she must be close to the dam where Mack had been trapped.

I hesitated to leave the baby's side to tell Penny where I was, and I had to hope she was asleep with the remaining eight young ones instead of worrying about my absence.

My hope was dashed when I saw her tail splash as she entered the pond to try to find me.

"What are you doing?" she asked me as she emerged onto the bank and shook herself off. She looked exhausted and I realized then that she could not, of course, sleep while her son was missing.

"I'm watching Beej," I told her. "Livia has gone to help Mack."

"Really?" she asked as she sidled up beside me and the baby. "She left her baby with you to do that?"

"Yes, she did," I nodded, and added, "We are all connected."

"Family. Yes, we are," she said, gazing at the baby. "Look, though, she's already bigger than our little kits."

It was true—although our kits would keep growing throughout their lives instead of stopping like humans did after they became adults.

I thought about Mack then, who was about half the size he would be a year later when he would be ready to leave us.

If he hadn't already left us, I thought. No, that was wrong. Taken from us. Stolen. Trapped.

I shook my head and scratched my ears to clear those thoughts from my head.

Just then, Beej began to cry.

Penny turned to me. "Oh, that's not good," she said, and I knew she was thinking what I was – that the sound of a human cry could attract the attention of other humans – and animal predators, too.

"What should we do?" Penny asked.

I had an idea. I didn't know if she would like it. But I took a chance.

"Nurse her?" I said softly.

Penny wrinkled her eyes at me. I knew she was considering the implications of this for the baby. Was it healthy? Would it work? What would it mean for the bond between them?

"Family," she said again and rolled next to the baby, adjusting her belly so Beej could reach one of her four teats. She used her front paws to move the baby's mouth gently toward her, careful not to scratch her with her claws, murmured encouragingly, and waited.

It worked! I watched as Beej's mouth and cheeks worked back and forth as I'd seen each one of our kits do, and she did the same swallowing action and gulping for breath from time to time, too.

We really were family now.

Penny closed her eyes briefly. I knew she was tired. I admired her so for the way she had fed and loved all our kits—and now this baby—so unselfishly and yet with a strength that astounded me.

She was giving generously of herself even in her grief and worry. Just as she had always done with each kit in all our litters.

191

Her name was Kitty.

She was the larger of our fourth litter of two. Even though Penny and I were raising our fourth litter, I thought back on how young and inexperienced we were – even more so because there was so much that we didn't know that we didn't know.

Kitty came first, and then Scout. Our two first newborn kits after the flood that had destroyed so much. It felt like a new beginning when they were born. At least, we'd hoped it was.

Kitty had a feline look about her, with eyes that were more pecan in shape than acorn, and that's how she got her name. And her brother was born curious, even in his first nights, trying to slide down the main entrance of the lodge to enter the water. That was why we called him Scout.

We delighted in their every move as they nursed and learned to float and then swim and dive, as we showed them how to eat the lily pads and roots and green duckweed. They were hard workers and enjoyed the harvesting of trees with us, proud as the year went on and their teeth grew long enough to advance to harder wood.

They were a year old when we took them to a nearby pond one night. I'd seen some maples nearby that I thought they would like. I blamed myself for this later.

As we rose from the water of the adjacent pond to access the bank of maples, Kitty was caught in a trap that came down on her back, and if that wasn't horrible enough, as she tried to wiggle away, it dragged her underwater and held her there so long that she could no longer breathe.

I recalled again how great our grief was on that day. Penny and I were never the same. We became stricter parents with all our kits, admonishing them, lecturing them, watching over them as closely as we could.

Scout suffered under our constant attention, and when the next year was up, he gladly left us to find his own territory.

We had never lost another kit, though, so in some way, perhaps Kitty had helped us become better parents to all the kits that came after her.

Until now.

I watched as Penny nursed Beej and the baby grew full and sleepy as her mouth moved more slowly. I knew she would be quiet now for a long time as our newborn kits were after a good, rich meal.

Eventually, her mouth grew slack, and she moved away from Penny's body, breathing peacefully.

Penny repositioned herself to sit up next to me, and we gazed out upon the pond. The sun was past the midway point, and I couldn't remember the last time we'd stayed up this late during the day.

We stayed still and listened for any stirrings from the eight kits still in the lodge, but all was quiet, and that was a relief. We swiveled our ears in the direction of the big dam, hoping against hope to hear someone coming.

There was a rustling, but it was simply a squirrel scrambling up a tree in that frantic way they do.

Just at the moment when the sun tipped down toward the horizon and created the shimmering gold lines of afternoon upon the water, right when I was about to give up hope, we heard something.

My heart leapt, and Penny ran into the water.

I stayed next to Beej, faithful to the charge I'd made to her mother. But my whole being was in that pond as I watched my partner and our son rolling and hugging and splashing and squealing with joy as they reunited with each other.

Mack was back!

Even my gigantic orange teeth were no match for my grin of happiness.

Soon Mack swam over to me, and Penny resumed her position by the baby so I could greet my son.

"Papa," he cried with tears falling, unafraid to show emotion after what he had been through. "I'm so sorry I couldn't do what you suggested and chew my foot from the trap to get loose."

"Son," I said to him. "There is no need to apologize. You did what you felt was right. And that is always the best thing to do."

I kissed his cheek and groomed him on his back and behind his ears, and then inspected his paw. It had bled a bit but was already healing. I would gather some willow for him after Livia returned.

And then it struck me: where was Livia?

My stomach sunk in dread.

"Mack," I said. "Did you see Livia?"

"Yes," he said. "She was the one who unlatched the lock from the trap."

"So where is she?"

"There was a man," he said. "She stayed to face him down. So I could be free."

Livia

"Hey, that was my beaver!"

My heart was pounding as I faced him, but I stood strong and yelled back, "He was not *your* beaver!"

My eyes scanned down to his hands that still held one end of the pole with the net he'd intended to use to carry Mack away.

"And you won't be needing that net either," I snarled, looking to his pockets for evidence of a knife or other weapons.

"Livia?" he said, his tone suddenly softer.

I turned my eyes from his pockets to his face, which was shaded by the cap he was wearing.

"Grayson?" I asked.

He nodded.

"You look so different now," he said.

"You do, too," I replied. He was so much thinner. He looked ten years older than he had the last time I saw him, which had been only a few weeks ago.

Of course, I was thinner, too, and the fact that he noticed that about my body made me nervous. It meant he would know I'd had the baby. I was anxious to get back to her.

I decided to try being nice, although there was a large part of me that still wanted to pummel him for trapping the beaver.

"Want to sit for a moment?" I asked.

He nodded and sat so quickly I thought he might fall out. He did look so pale and weak. I guessed he was incredibly hungry and that was why he'd tried to capture Mack.

"How have you been?" I asked gently.

He took his cap off his head and tilted his head back and stared up at the sun through the frond-like branches of hickory leaves.

"Not so good," he said. I remembered he'd always been quieter than his loquacious dad and that made me wonder why he was alone out here.

"My dad is gone," he said as if in answer to my unasked question.

"Oh, Grayson, I'm so sorry," I responded. "I know what that's like. I lost my family, too."

"Even your aunt?" he asked, bending his head down from the trees to look at me.

"There never was an aunt," I found myself saying. It was unexpected, this turn toward truth in me. I guessed I was simply tired of running and stealing and lying. From him. From everything.

"Oh," he said softly, realizing I had lied to him and his dad. "So why didn't you come with us on that day?"

I realized that not only was he incredibly hungry, out here in the woods as he was, hoping to catch a beaver to eat—but he was also desperately lonely.

I wasn't sure how to respond. I didn't want to lie anymore. But the whole truth about why I'd told Rusty and Grayson that I had an aunt and why I hadn't trusted them enough to stay with them at that moment was more than I could bring myself to say.

"Bad things happened," I said finally. "I wasn't ready to trust anyone."

He simply looked at me kindly with his soft brown eyes but said nothing. He waited until I was ready to speak again.

"This whole thing is so bizarre," I said. It felt good to say it. I hadn't had anyone to talk to about what had happened to the world. "Sometimes I still can't believe it's all real."

"Don't I know it," he responded.

I took a leap then – I leapt like the fish that he and his dad had helped me catch on the day I met them, the food they helped provide for me that probably had helped save my life – and the life of my baby.

"I had my baby," I said.

His face broke into a grin suddenly. "Really? That's great." But then he grew serious and asked, "Where is she?"

I took a deep breath. It was another terrifying leap, a trapeze artist type of jump without a net. But I was ready to trust someone. The beavers were teaching me again how to do that.

"I've been living with her out here in the forest near a beaver pond. That's why I was so mad about the trap. The beavers have become our friends. More than that. They are our family. One of them is guarding my baby right now."

I did not know if he would think I was crazy. I wasn't even sure if I cared if he did.

"No way!" he said, slapping his knee with his hand and laughing.

"Yes way," I answered, smiling a bit as I remembered that this was an expression Mouse often used to say.

"Well, I guess it makes sense now that you wouldn't want me to eat your family."

I had to laugh out loud at that. "That's for sure!" I giggled.

I looked at the sun tilting down in the direction of the river. I remembered the red kayak that had brought me there, and the steamboat I saw – so inexplicably wacky – and wondered where Grayson was staying. If there were more humans nearby.

I took another chance and asked him. "Where have you been staying?"

"After my dad was gone, I lived for a while back at our house. The fires missed our neighborhood because it was across the river away from the city. But it was just too weird to be there alone."

"I know what you mean."

"So I packed up as much of our fishing and hunting and camping gear that I could carry in a big Army backpack my dad had and I crossed the river by foot using an old railroad bridge on a dark moon night. I decided that deep into the woods would be the safest place to settle. I didn't really trust anyone and didn't want to go any closer into the city. Especially after the fire."

I nodded. No explanation necessary.

"That's very similar to my story," I said.

He turned his cap around in his hands as if it held a clue to what he wanted to say next. Then he rubbed his hand across his face, which was clean shaven. He must have a razor, I thought. I wondered what other tools he might also have. I remembered how shy he'd been when I first met him, and what a boisterous and joking man his father had been. It must have been a very quiet life without him.

"Listen," I said. "Would you like to come with me to the beaver pond? And meet my daughter? I've been away from her for so long. And she must be hungry."

I saw his eyes flicker briefly to register what I meant by how I knew she was hungry.

"Thank you kindly," he said. "I could use the company."

"Okay," I said. "But leave all that here." I pointed to the trap still on the ground and the net sitting beside him. I never wanted to see either thing again, but the least I could do was to demand that he not bring them to the pond.

We walked back through the woods, and as we did, I noticed how the forest did indeed feel like home to me. The comfortable way my feet knew how to go. The bends in the creek and the trees were familiar to me after only a month out there.

And when I sensed the pond ahead, I stopped.

"Wait here," I said to Grayson and pointed to a large rock. "Sit and I will come back to you soon."

He did as I said.

I walked slowly toward the pond in the east. Chap was still there near the shelter, and Penny was next to him. Beej was not crying with hunger but was sleeping peacefully, much to my surprise.

I could see the beavers as they twitched their snouts to smell the strange human out of sight behind me.

"I found a friend," I said to them as I approached the shelter. "He has lost his family like me. I think we can trust him."

"I'm not sure about this," Chap said.

"Me, either," said Penny.

"I understand," I responded. "Particularly after what you've just been through with Mack. That's why I left him there. So I could talk with you first. See what you thought. Ask your permission."

They looked at each other in silent communication.

"Okay," Penny said. "You can bring him here to your shelter. But I am not ready to show him my kits or myself until I have time to observe him."

"I agree," said Chap. "It's too soon. And we need to sleep anyway. We don't have much time until the sun sets and we must get up for work. We will go back to the lodge and then you can bring him here."

"Thank you," I said. "I understand your hesitation. And I will respect your wishes. I will keep him near the shelter and away from the lodge."

At that, they waddled toward the shore, and I called to them, "And thank you for watching over Beej!"

"You're very welcome. And thank you for helping Mack return to us!" whistled Penny before they dove into the pond together.

Chap

What a day it had been. A terrifying night and an endless, sleepless day. And now it was almost night again.

I lay in the lodge, watching the light becoming more golden, still anxious and reflecting on all that had happened. The pride I felt in my yearlings as we'd worked together on the big dam the night before: that seemed like a year ago to me now.

The fear still coursing through me from seeing Mack in a trap—this was why I was not sleeping. The reverberations of terror at that.

The horror on the faces of Henry and Gigi as they had to say goodbye to their brother.

The wailing their mother did when I told her the news.

It was all too much for a beaver to take.

But then the trade I made with Livia – that she would go to rescue my son while I protected her daughter. And the way Penny had joined us and nursed the baby.

Oh, my mind spun with the wonder of it all!

I saw the image again of Penny and Beej, like mother and daughter, but from different species. Could members of different species also be in the same family? Would Penny and I ever tell Livia what we had done?

And now there was another human – and a male. It surprised me, quite honestly, that Livia would bring a male to our pond. That she would want to show him her shelter. Introduce him to her daughter. Did this mean her loyalties were still more aligned with the human world? I wondered.

I looked over at Mack in the waning light. He was home. He had returned to us. Livia had helped him escape and now he was safe. Those were the most important things. And I was grateful. That wouldn't have been possible without Livia's help.

I was finally beginning to let the waves of tension from the day recede and was feeling pleasantly sleepy when I noticed Gigi wriggling to wake.

"Mack!" she squealed in delight when she saw her brother.

This woke the others, and they all piled on him, kissing on him, nuzzling each other with joy, grooming one another and generally wiggling around in gladness as kits will do.

There would be no sleep for me today, after all, I realized. But my heart was happy to see my whole family together again.

Penny felt the same way, too, I could tell, as she moved her body closer to me and we watched them.

"What happened, Mack?" Henry asked. "How did you get free?"

"Did you chew your foot?" Gigi asked, trying to see.

"Was it very scary?" mewed Mick to the older brother who had given him his name.

Meadow chimed in, too, and said, "How did you do it? Please tell us."

The truth was that Penny and I wanted to hear the story, too.

"Well," started Mack. "I decided not to chew off my foot even though it seemed like my only chance for survival. At first, I thought I was being cowardly for deciding not to do this. But I thought about what it would be like to live without a foot. I remembered how long it took for my tail to heal after the tree fell on it. The pain, night after night, and even day after day when it throbbed in my sleep and hurt so much that I lay awake in agony. I didn't want to go through all that again."

We all listened attentively.

"And then I smelled a human."

Gem breathed in sharply in fear.

"I tried to sense if they were far or near, stranger or familiar. But honestly, I was so exhausted from being trapped that my sense of smell was bad."

I saw Henry instinctively wrinkle his nose with displeasure at the prospect of losing our strongest, most protective sense.

"It was Livia!" Mack said dramatically.

"Livia!?" they all cried simultaneously.

"Yes. She was the one who freed me. She figured out how to unlatch the lock. And my leg came free."

"Oh, my goodness!" Gaia sighed.

"But then there was another human," continued Mack.

"What?" shouted Hero.

"Hush," I said. "Not so loud." It was near the time when we would need to leave the lodge to eat, and I didn't want them to attract attention with their sounds.

"Sorry," said Hero more quietly. "But Mack, there was another human?"

"Yes," Mack answered. "And you should have seen Livia. She stood up angrily like we do when we get on our hind legs to protect our territory. She was so fierce I could have sworn she grew beaver teeth."

Meadow and Gem giggled.

"She stopped the man from coming closer to me. She gave me time to escape. I ran straight for the lake by the big dam as fast as I could. I swam home faster than I ever thought I would. And Papa and Mama were there, near her shelter, waiting to welcome me."

They all sighed with relief at the ending of the story.

And then little Happy, who had been quietly listening, riveted the whole time, finally spoke.

"I'm so happy!" he chirped.

Everyone laughed and the kits started to roll and wrestle and play with delight once again.

It was time for me to do my evening inspection. The light through the air hole glowed with crimson. But before I left, I went over to Mack and pressed my chin upon the top of his head. I stayed still like that, and when I did, all the others settled down, motionless, watching. This is a great honor for the motion is one of absolute trust as the most vulnerable part of the body, the throat, is closest to our fiercest weapon, our sharp and gigantic orange front teeth.

I was telling him, in that gesture, that I honored him deeply. I was proud of him. I trusted him. I was deeply thankful that he was alive. And that he was home. My heart was glad that he was my son.

Livia

Was I making a mistake?

I wondered this about this even as I picked up Beej and went forward to where Grayson was waiting. I considered it. Like a pebble in my shoe, it dug into my foot.

The grin on his face, though, allowed me to tell myself everything would be okay. He could be trusted.

"I had a sister," he said, his eyes glowing as he looked at Beej and then at me. "She was younger. I remember her being this tiny when I was a kid."

"I had a sister, too," I told him. "But I didn't know her as a baby. She came into my life later."

In this way, we began to know each other by offering bits of who we used to be. Like Hansel and Gretel, the crumbs led us back to a sense of home with each other in the forest. Small parts of what we remembered. Those we had lost. Together, we started to work out who we could still be.

We walked back to the shelter and sat under it as we faced the pond and watched the setting crimson sun playing with the soft ripples of green and gold upon the pond as it was reflecting the day's last light.

"Her name was Megan," he told me. "Named after our mother. She was eleven years younger than me. That's why I can remember what she was like as a baby. Oh, she was the apple of everybody's eye, that's for sure. Bright blue eyes, blonde hair soft as cotton candy. And sweet, too. Wouldn't hurt a fly."

At this, his brown eyes clouded over.

"We stayed healthy longer than most families, I guess. We lived out in the country west of the river so we could stay away from other people at first and order what we needed to be delivered. As long as the supply chains were up and running."

I nodded. I knew what he was saying was harder for him to say than it was for me to hear, and I also knew, from experience, the relief he would feel from telling the story.

"It was the second summer. August. A year ago." He shook his head. "I sometimes can't believe time anymore. That first year went so fast, the news updates and everybody on edge. And then this past year, it was like everything became molasses."

"I know what you mean," I told him. I knew he was swimming around the heart of the story. I let him take his time.

"One morning, my dad woke and realized that he was plum out of feed for the chickens. He blamed himself. He was usually very organized and ordered extra even when he didn't think we'd need it. But it slipped his mind. And the chickens, their eggs, they kept us going."

I found my mouth watering at the thought of fresh scrambled eggs for breakfast.

"My mom didn't want him to go, begged him to stay, but he insisted we had stayed well so far because of the nutrition the daily eggs gave us."

Rusty struck me as someone who would sooner die than fail to provide for his family, and I told Grayson so.

His eyes filled with tears. "I believe you're right," he said. "And that would have been fine, except that Megan, who was six years old at the time, begged him to let her tag along, saying she was dying from boredom after months of not going anywhere."

He stopped. I knew what was coming and I didn't want to know.

"So he let her go with him. An older woman at the feed store came up to Megan while they waited in the line to check out. She exclaimed, 'It's been so long since I've seen a little girl!' And then she touched her arm."

I flinched instinctively and held Beej a bit more tightly.

"Of course, my dad made her get directly into the shower as soon as they got home," he continued. "But it was too late. She was dead within a week."

"I'm so sorry," I said, almost whispering.

It was painful to listen to him tell the story, as the memory came back to me of Mouse walking into my room that summer morning and saying, "Livia, I've spiked a fever."

"No, you haven't," I had said. It came out meaner than I'd intended.

Her eyes, glassy and bloodshot, stared at me. She knew the truth in her body, no matter how I tried to deny it.

"I'm going to my room," she said. "I'm going to lock the door." Her eyes filled with tears. "Can you tell my mother for me, please? I can't do it. It would be too hard not to let her hug me one last time."

"Don't say that!" I said, but she had already turned and was walking down the hall to her bedroom. I heard the latch turning. I thought of the latch I'd unlocked for Mack that very day. I wished I could turn back time and do everything differently. That was the last time I saw my best friend. My sister.

Katrina respected Mouse's wishes and let her stay in her room. She delivered meals to her outside her door, leaving them on the floor on paper plates with plastic utensils and a small trash bag that Mouse could put everything into, which Katrina would pick up later and take directly to the trash bin outside, wearing gloves. That was when the garbage trucks were still coming regularly.

Sometimes Katrina sat on the floor in the hallway and talked softly to Mouse inside, telling her stories from when she was young, things Kat wanted her to remember about what they'd done together or how cute and funny Mouse had been.

I stayed in my room, my earbuds on, trying not to listen. So incredibly strong in me was the tendency to try to pretend. The cell towers and electrical grids were still working then so I could escape that way with music and technology.

Mouse's final wish was granted, and none of us got sick from her. She died alone, in her room, and we didn't see her again until the first responders, covered from head to toe in yellow hazmat suits, crashed open her door to take away her body.

That was when there were still ambulances and first responders.

"By the time Mouse's mom got sick that winter," I told Grayson. "So much had changed. The cell phone towers had been destroyed by rival gangs, and there were already fuel shortages so no ambulance would have come if we'd been able to call anyway."

He nodded, remembering.

"Mouse's mom was also my mom," I told him. It was important to me that he knew this. I could not trust him if I kept this part of my past secret. I saw his face registering what he was telling me, but he did not flinch as I'd sometimes seen other people do.

"She and my mom met when Mouse and I were toddlers," I told him. "At first, they were just friends. Best friends. And then more. They fell in love. They got married when we were six years old."

It struck me then – what I was saying.

"We were the same age as Megan," I said softly. "It all seems like a dream to me now. Mouse and I wore matching bridesmaid's dresses. Lavender.

Their favorite color. We all carried bouquets of lavender they ordered from an island off Washington State."

How easily something like matching lavender dresses could be ordered so easily. How something as rare and beautiful as fragile flowers could be delivered across the continent back then. How much we'd taken for granted.

"Kat was a biologist at the university. She knew about the virus before most people did. She warned us. Tried to prepare us. But it was so hard to believe that everything would come crashing down as quickly as it did."

"I know what you mean," he said. "Things had been hard for so long that we kind of got used to it. We got used to the masks and the social distancing with the earlier viruses. We heard on the news about the chaos erupting in other countries. The breakdowns of governments. The lack of food. We just didn't think it would happen here."

I nodded, agreeing with him. Remembering the news on in the middle of the night blasting from Katrina's laptop as it lay propped up between her and my mom in bed when I got up to go to the bathroom. Putting in my earbuds and turning up my music to drown out the sound of it.

"We thought we were special," I said.

"We did," he said.

I took a deep breath and shifted Beej from one arm to another. Already the muscles around my shoulder had healed from my fall. How resilient the body was, I thought. Until it wasn't.

"My mom and I woke up one morning and Katrina was gone. She knew, as a biologist, what would happen to her body once the virus made its way in. She left us a note. It was mostly a love note to my mother."

I stopped. My voice caught in tears. I had never said any of this out loud before. When it happened, the only ones left were my mother and me. There had been no one else to tell.

Grayson lifted his hand and placed it upon my shoulder. Lightly. Hesitating.

I let him keep it there.

I kept talking as the sun went down over the pond and I nursed Beej.

"They loved each other so much. I didn't think my mom would survive the grief. She ran out the front door of the house to look for Kat, but there was no way to know where she had gone. We had a quarter tank of gas left in the truck, and I knew my mom wanted to save it for emergencies. I watched her as she ran down the street screaming Katrina's name. Hoping she would be just around a corner and come back to her. Change her mind somehow. Say she'd made a mistake. I knew my mom loved her so much that she wouldn't have cared about the virus. She would have stayed next to Kat for as long as she could, feeding her soup and bringing her water and putting cold towels on her forehead as the fever raged."

"My mom did that for my sister," Grayson said softly. "Never left her alone for a minute. And got sick soon after."

I reached over with my right arm as I cradled Beej against me with my left, and I took his hand from my shoulder.

And held it. Skin to skin.

It was the first real human contact I'd initiated in longer than I wanted to remember. The memory came back to me of the day I placed my hand against the plexiglass of my mother's hospital room. The cold flatness of it.

The sun had gone down completely, and it was too dark to see, but I heard him crying softly next to me as we held hands.

I felt the warm relief of tears running down my cheeks, too. And the warmth of his hand in mine.

And then we lay back upon the ground on our sides, still holding hands and facing Beej as she lay between us.

And we cried ourselves to sleep.

When I woke, he was gone.

I'd slept more soundly than I had since I first arrived there, but this time, without nightmares to interrupt me.

I sat up and looked around for him. I felt a slight panic and wanted to go look for him, but Beej was fussing and hungry. I held her to my breast and watched the peach light of dawn playing on the water's surface.

I missed him already. How was this possible? I missed him in the same fierce way I'd not hesitated to go help Mack when I learned he'd been trapped.

I had made a mistake, I realized, but it hadn't been in coming to the forest, or even in inviting Grayson to be with me the day before. I had been wrong to let Mouse walk away from me that day. My arms ached, even as they held Beej against me, to be able hug Mouse once more. And Katrina. And my mom.

Penny swam to me near the shore.

"Where is your friend?" she asked.

"I don't know. I woke up and he was gone."

"Do you think he will come back?"

I shook my head. "I don't know."

She waddled up to me, gently patted Beej, and said, "I remember when I first met Chap."

My eyebrows shot up. I hadn't expected this. She'd been so skeptical of Grayson's presence the day before.

"He was young and alone," she continued. "He was, as he is now, eager and earnest. But since he was younger, he was also afraid, and maybe tried too hard to please me."

We looked to the water where we could see him swimming with the kits as they headed back to the lodge to sleep.

"But he was trustworthy," she said. "That was the most important thing. Beavers mate for life, so I had to be able to know I could trust him with mine. And with the lives of our kits."

I nodded. I already felt the same way about Grayson. I could leave Beej with him if I had to – I trusted him that much.

"I watched you both sleeping last night with the baby between you," she said. "I did not smell any malice on him."

I thought about Mack and the trap, and the net Grayson had been carrying when I first saw him. I wondered if she knew about that.

"They must be trained. That's what I'm saying," she said to me. "They don't know everything at first. It comes gradually."

We heard rustling in the forest, and she nodded at me. "He can stay here," she said quickly. And then she dove into the water to join Chap and their kits.

I turned away from the pond to see Grayson standing in front of the shelter holding the bottom of his green t-shirt with both of his hands.

"I got us breakfast," he said smiling, and tipped the shirt to show me – mushrooms!

"How did you find them?" I asked. I'd been craving them and remembered my mom and Kat would forage for them out here when we went camping, but I hadn't had any luck finding some.

"You just have to know where to look," he said, placing them gently onto the ground and then taking two green branches and skewering them one at a time.

I thought about what Penny had just said to me as Grayson piled pine straw and dried twigs into the firepit and lit it.

"What are you grinning about?" he said. He was also smiling.

"I knew kids at school who did shrooms on a date, but I don't think this is what they meant," I said.

"This is a date?" The light in his deep brown eyes twinkled with the lemony yellow light of the late summer morning sun behind me, and he reminded me of Chap.

"Sure is," I joked. "You haven't heard about the breakfast date craze? It's the latest trend. All the rage with the social media influencers. The internet is blowing up about it."

He laughed and shook his head. "The internet sure did blow up, didn't it?"

"Yes, it did," I said, and I chuckled. It was the first time I'd been able to make a joke about anything in a very long time.

"I sure don't miss all of that mess," he said.

"Me, neither," I said. And I meant it.

Chap

There was a stone formation near the river where I'd first met Penny, and as I lay in the lodge with our kits all around us that morning, the memory of it came back to me.

A large rock rose from the ground, as tall as three beavers and with a long, wide back like we have. That kind of considerable outcropping of stone wasn't unusual in our forest, especially so close to the river.

But on top of that were two smaller, longish stones that lay together like branches from a tree. Gray and white stripes and flecks of sunny yellow ran through them. And it was on that foundational sculpture shaped by nature itself that I nuzzled against Penny for the first time.

I'd gotten her scent a few nights previously and started making patties with mud and leaving my fragrance on them to show her I was nearby. I knew she would have to be the one to approach me. Otherwise, I would be perceived as too aggressive.

It was close to sundown, and I was on that rock watching the golden sun leaking lemony cream onto the river before it turned to the sweet gold and amber of honeyed light, and this was when I first saw her.

She swam up and created citrine circles in the water as her small snout reached up to sniff and greet me with a soft whistle. I felt like the luckiest beaver in the world.

Her coat was shiny with flecks of smoky cinnamon as she dried herself on the bank and then scrambled up onto the rock to join me.

I inhaled her scent, and it became part of me.

We had not left each other's side for longer than we needed in order to work and build and gather food ever since. I had lost count of how many winters we'd lodged together, but I knew we were on our ninth litter of kits.

This, too, was what was happening with the humans, I knew.

The edge of the pond that Penny and I had created together through the construction of our dams was like that rock formation for them – the place that held their bodies as they created a foundation for what would come next.

Days and nights went by like this, as they foraged and fished during the day while we slept, and then at sunset, we exchanged places and ventured out together, all eleven of us, to process the poplars I'd found the night that Livia had fallen.

Her wounds were healing well, I could tell, as we passed them, sleeping, her knees curled up to make a nest for the baby and him snuggled behind her with his arms around her. There would be scars, but her skin was recovering.

Our bodies are resilient, I thought, even though they are so vulnerable. I had always thought of humans as a kind of terrible beast, only out to destroy and take whatever they wanted. But watching this little human family from so close, I realized the fragility we shared in common.

We both loved and wanted to express that love.

We both gathered what we ate and wanted to share it with our families.

We both created shelters and wanted to protect our loved ones who lived in them.

As the nights went by and the days grew shorter, I witnessed how they worked together to add to their structure. He left for a long time one night under a dark moon and returned with more pieces of metal. Not traps, thank goodness, but sharp metal things they used to process larger pieces of wood to make walls and smaller metal things they used to attach a door and a roof to their lodge.

They were getting ready for winter just as we did, I realized.

And as we added to our cache of food under water, they used some of the metal containers he'd carried back to treat the fish and other foods that they foraged so it would last longer.

Together, both of us realized the great gifts that the trees gave us. For us, the trees provided food and shelter, not to mention the ability to create dams that enabled the water lands to exist and the water tables below the land to grow wider and deeper for times when it was drier. For humans, the trees offered shelter as well as heat for warmth and cooking.

Both our kits were growing, too, I noticed. Beej was beginning to pay attention to the things around her and reach for sticks to hold in her fingers, which bent and curled upon each other like the paws of our kits did, but with the addition of a little thumb instead of a fifth claw.

She did not cry as much as she had when she was first born, either, and one evening, as I left the lodge to do my inspection, I heard her baby laughter reverberating across the water.

We never saw a trap again for as long as they were near us.

And for this, I was thankful.

The leaves upon the trees were dressed in their dancing colors that they wore right before the arrival of winter. I sometimes stayed awake, floating just outside the entrance to the lodge a little longer than usual at that time of year to watch their red and gold and orange shapes as they swayed together in the morning light and leapt down to the ground one at a time in their final embrace of earth.

It was early on a morning like this, while the humans were still asleep in the cozy cabin that they'd built, with the smoke from their stone chimney rising to meet the cold sunlight, that I smelled something alarming.

My snout went up into the air to ascertain better what was coming.

Human. Meat eaters. A sour kind of something was emanating from them, too. I slapped my tail against the water to make a whacking, warning sound.

I heard the silence from within the lodge as my family registered what I meant by that signal and stayed still and quiet for protection.

I slid into the entrance as quickly as I could.

And listened.

Voices. Human. Male.

I tried to count how many there were by distinguishing one from the other, but I lost count. I heard the words "smoke" and "cabin" and "nice." I felt the reverberations of their footsteps echoing from the ground to the water and then landing upon my body, and deeper even, into my heart.

I felt the vibrations from Grayson's footsteps, too, as he moved within their shelter.

I heard the soft cry of the baby, and Livia's attempt to shush her.

Their cabin door opened with a slight squeak from the metal pieces, and I heard Grayson walk out to greet the new humans after shutting the door behind him.

I heard another metal clanking behind the door as Livia put the lock into place as Grayson had told her to do. To protect herself and the baby.

"Hey, how's it going?" Grayson asked them.

"Nice place you got there," one of the strangers said.

"Yes, it is," Grayson answered.

I heard in his voice that he was trying to determine if they were predators. It was harder for humans to know this at first because their bodies are all the same. For us, an otter is an otter. A wolf and fox and coyote are wolf and fox and coyote. We know right away what we are dealing with by being able to depend upon our smell and sight.

Humans can't always count on words, either. Many of them, Livia and Grayson had told me, use language to say one thing and mean another. They taught me that they must discern the intentions from the tones of voice, like they learned to do to communicate with us.

I wished I could help. I wanted to watch at least. Be closer. Sniff the humans out and share the information I gathered with Grayson. I felt weak and helpless in the darkened lodge. But my family was safe. And I couldn't risk ruining that security.

I saw Penny's copper eyes widen as she listened, too. The kits were frozen in place, not because we admonished them to do so, but from a predisposition deep within them.

We had to stay where we were. In the safety of our lodge in the water. That was our only option.

And wait.

Livia

"Liv? Liv? Wake up."

Grayson shook me from sleep and whispered urgently. I looked around me at the cabin we'd built together.

It had taken us weeks, Grayson and I working together when the baby was sleeping, and separately when she was awake. He'd found a pile of pallets behind an abandoned warehouse on one of his excursions back to his childhood home, and he'd used the wheelbarrow to bring them one at a time to our pond. There, we dismantled them, carefully saving as many nails as we could salvage to be reused in the construction. First, he designed a frame with the 2 x 4 sections of the pallets. Piece by piece, we arranged the boards horizontally, nailing each of them to the frame. We opted not to create windows, but he did go back to his home to take the hinges off the doors from the front, side, and back of the house, and he brought these doors and all their hinges back to us to finish the construction by creating a roof and door. This resulted in a low-ceilinged, snug, and secure home for us.

Small shafts of sunlight were coming through a few cracks in the eastern walls, so I knew it was morning, but Beej was still and peaceful in her little homemade cradle by our bed on the floor which we'd made by piling dozens of the quilts his mother had made and the blankets she'd crocheted over her lifetime.

Why then did Grayson sound so worried?

"People are near," he whispered. "I'm going to check it out. Stay here. Lock the door."

Beej fussed a bit in her sleep as he was pulling on jeans and a sweater he'd brought from his old house, and I leaned over to pick her up and comfort her.

He turned once to kiss us both. "Stay here," he whispered to me. "I mean it."

There was so much I wanted to say. But he was already out the door. I took a deep breath and let it out slowly as I pulled the latch on the door as quietly as I could with one hand while holding Beej in the other. And listened.

"Hey, how's it going?" I heard him ask.

"Nice place you got there," one of them said. I guessed from the sound of his voice that he was on the southern side of the pond.

"Yes, it is," Grayson answered, his voice further than it had been at first. He was trying to draw them away from us by going closer to them.

Us. Them. The ingredients for so much of what had happened in the past few years. And destroyed everything.

I paced back and forth on the dirt floor of the cabin a few times, bouncing Beej in my arms. I wanted to be with him. I didn't want to be locked up in a cabin with no windows holding a baby. I felt the adrenaline coursing through my veins as it had when Katrina first came home with news of another virus. And when Mouse walked into my room to say she had a fever. And when the bitter cold entered my house that winter morning. And when I went to chop wood. And after. And that last morning I woke in my own bed, smelling smoke and knowing I'd have to leave my house forever the flee the fires.

Smoke. Fire. Us. Them.

I put Beej into her cradle and tried shaking myself all over, as I'd seen the beavers do to clear their fear. But she fussed again, and I didn't want anyone to hear her, so I picked her up and crawled back on top of the piled quilts to nurse her.

And listened again. I couldn't hear anything except the rustling of dry leaves in the wind and the morning birdsong as endlessly optimistic as ever.

If it weren't for Beej, I would have opened the door. If it weren't for her, I wouldn't have let Grayson leave without me in the first place.

I tried to think about what else I could do, but my mind was jammed up like a bad radio signal.

Bits and pieces of thoughts. Feminism. Anger. Violence. Gender.

The design flaw of the slow growth of human babies and their long period of infancy.

"It's what allows the human brain to develop in such complex ways," Katrina had said once at dinner after Mouse asked her why it took so long for children to grow up. "The longer a species stays with its mother, the more time it has to learn."

And then I heard a gunshot. And another.

My breath left me, and I turned cold. Beej stopped nursing and swung her head back to look at my face.

I was afraid to pass on my terror to her, so I forced myself to smile. Closed mouth. No teeth. I felt tears welling up in my eyes.

Shouting.

"Cut it out!"

"Make me!"

Laughter.

One of the voices was Grayson's.

I stood up and put Beej down into her cradle again. I couldn't stay there. I couldn't just wait. After all I'd been through. I got dressed in some clothes Grayson brought me that had been his when he was a few years younger. Black corduroy pants and a long-sleeved undershirt. Then a wool sweater his mother had knit for him.

I looked at Beej one more time and then unlocked the door.

Footsteps. Running. Coming this way. I quickly relocked the latch and stood there.

"Liv?" I heard Grayson whispering breathlessly from the other side of the door. "It's me."

"Finally!" I said, throwing open the door and pulling him inside before locking it again. "What happened?"

"Some guys," he said, catching his breath. "They smelled like they'd been drinking all night. They said there's a steamboat on the river that sells liquor. Gambling. Girls. It docked nearby on the river overnight, and after drinking until sunrise, they decided to go hunting. All jacked up." He shook his head.

"And the gunshots?" I asked.

"One of them shot at the beaver lodge."

I stood frozen with fury.

"The bullets ricocheted off the water," he said. "So dangerous. But they missed the lodge. Steamboat punks. Dumb asses."

"What are we going to do?" I asked. "Can we stay here now that they know we are here?"

I looked around at the little home we had built. I had thought it was safe, this far from the roads. And people.

I thought of the steamboat I'd seen on my first day in the forest. It had been so bizarre, and I'd been so hungry that I assumed I may have imagined it. There was no way to get news from the outside world without risking our lives, and this lack of information had given me the illusion that we were too far away for anyone to bother us.

I'd been wrong.

Grayson was angry and showing it. I could almost see smoke coming out of his ears like in the old cartoons Mouse and I watched on television on Saturday mornings. I went over and put my hand on his shoulder.

"Look," I said. "It's not up to you alone to protect us. That's bullshit. I won't stand for it. I was losing it, sitting here with you out there and me in here. We can't do that again."

He nodded slowly.

"Where did they go?" I asked.

"Back to the steamboat to sleep it off, I guess."

"Okay," I said. Think, think, I said to myself. But when the next words came out of Grayson's mouth, I realized it wasn't thinking that would help me at that moment.

"I think we need a gun," he said.

And I responded with pure feeling.

Chap

"I'm going," she said.

"Oh, no, you are not," I responded.

"We can't just let them come here and shoot at our lodge," Penny said, her eyes flashing brightly even with the scant morning light coming through the air hole.

"They missed," I said. And I bent my head to her, showing how much I honored her. "Please. Please. Don't go. You will be missed."

I sat up again and looked at our kits.

I knew how fierce she was when she had a litter to look after. I knew every strand of hair in her two layers of fur was on end, wanting to leave the lodge and defend our territory. But I also knew her orange front teeth, as long as they were and as easily as they were able to cut wood, were no match for a man with a gun. And more than one man at that.

"I can't raise them alone," I pleaded. "Stay. Please."

She closed her eyes and twitched her mouth. I heard her back teeth grinding. I knew she was angry. I could only hope that her anger would not overpower her love.

Love. Work is the highest form of love. That's the water way.

I thought about how much love and work we had given to humans over the years.

I remembered back to another season of autumn, beautiful like this one, that turned cold and stormy one night. The rain came down so hard that Penny and I huddled with that year's litter of three new ones and four older ones all night long in the lodge. Even from our hiding place, we could hear the sounds of human sirens and flying machines as cars and houses were washed away. But how much worse that flood would have been if we hadn't done all the work that we did to create the dams, which slowed the water more than the humans would ever know.

Or ever thank us for.

And then, after that flood, the next year brought a summer of drought. Our four older ones were off on their own by then, and I worried about them trying to establish their own territories during a time that was so dry and hot. I spent as little time as I could out of the water that year as my blubber was a hindrance in such unrelenting heat, even in the middle of the night.

The humans did not know, of course, how much worse it could have been if we had not been there. Our work on the water ways meant that our streams and ponds created a flow deep underground, and this hidden source allowed an abundance of fresh drinking water for the humans to pipe into their homes even when the air was parched and the heat relentless.

How much they had taken for granted. Cool air in their homes in the summer, warmth in the winter. The world as they built it was made for their needs—and theirs alone. They separated themselves from us and from the world they had forgotten that made their very existence itself possible. Even the fresh water they piped into their buildings was kept clean and pure by our efforts. That is, until their selfishness led to their destruction.

I had watched in the last few months as Livia and Grayson did what they could do plant seeds around their cabin, and how difficult it was for them to nurture them long enough to feed their family. Even in this, we had helped all of them, as our water ways expanded the growth zones for so many plants in the forest and beyond. Humans had forgotten even the simple magic of a small flower that attracted bees under the sun and moths at night to enable all the growing world to thrive in ways they could never have imagined.

Theirs was a species with failures of both observation and imagination. The fish in the water, not to mention the insect and amphibian and reptile life who lived with us there, and the waterfowl and songbirds, too – every one of these millions of beings depended on beavers to create homes and provide food for them.

And all the mammals, too – even wolves and foxes and bobcats and coyotes who were our predators – the work we did was the base of the structure that upheld their ability to live. We were generous like that.

But humans were not.

I had thought that having Livia and Beej and Grayson here might be a new beginning for all of us. These turns of moon that we had spent with them had lulled me, though, into forgetting the cruelty of the other members of the species called humankind. I had forgotten that not all of them were kind.

I didn't want Penny to make the same mistake.

Finally, I watched Penny as she lifted her left front paw to scratch at her ear. She always did that when she was thinking and trying to come to a decision about what to do next. And then I saw the muscles in her back relax. She settled down on all four haunches and let her belly sink into the floor of the lodge.

She had given me her answer.

She wouldn't go beyond our door. This time.

Livia

"We most definitely do not need a gun!" I screamed at Grayson.

He stepped back from me with his eyes wide. I think he might have been more afraid of me than he had been of the steamboat punks. He had certainly never seen me so angry.

I brought my hands up to my face.

"I'm sorry," I said. "I didn't mean to yell like that."

I sat down on our bed ashamed of my outburst. I reached up my hand to him, pulling him down to sit next to me. I took a deep breath, gathering up my feelings like dust in a windstorm and trying to make sense of them.

"Okay," I said, finally. "Hear me out. I have been on my own longer than you have."

"It's not a competition," he said. His mouth was quivering, and I knew he was hurt by how upset I'd been.

"I know that. Please. Just listen. What I am trying to say is that when I was alone, I had a lot of time to think about things. Not just the way things had been. What we'd all lost. I knew that, and there was not much I could do as a teenaged girl all alone on my own to help with any of that."

His eyes softened. He knew what had happened to me. He knew the beginnings of Beej. And he didn't blame me for what I'd done in return.

"But I thought a lot about the origins. How it had all started. Long before the power grids went down. Even before the new virus and the gangs people formed to defend themselves from touch after that."

I saw him wince slightly. Touch was his love language, I knew, and I also knew how hard it had been for him to watch his sister and then his mother leave for the hospital without hugging him and his father goodbye. And I also knew, because he had told me, that he had been left by his dad, too.

Grayson guessed that Rusty spiked a fever one night, and in an attempt to save his son's life, Grayson woke up one morning to find his father had simply vanished. Like Katrina had done. To try to save us. They disappeared.

Grayson was still here, though.

And in this way, his father had succeeded.

I was still there, too. So Katrina had accomplished her goal, as well.

And we had Beej. She was growing and gaining weight and glowing with health. I would do nothing to risk that.

"Grayson," I continued. "Those steamboat punks, as you called them, who came into the woods after a night of drinking. They're not worth it. There will always be jerks like that as long as there are humans. They had a gun, yes. And they shot at the beaver lodge. It's horrible. I agree with you. But we cannot let the fear of people like that change who we are. What we have here is too precious – too fragile – to risk."

He looked over at Beej, slumbering deep into her mid-morning nap, as I said this.

"Not just Beej. All of it. The beavers and the birds and the frogs. The clean water. The trees. The crickets at night and the cicadas in the day during the summer. How they grow quiet when it turns colder. The music of the leaves in a summer wind and their change of pitch as they turn and fall in autumn. All of this, I think, has been what has sustained us. It's why we survived. And if we let one little incident with some drunken losers turn us into people with guns, then we've lost. We let ourselves become one of them. Can you see that?"

I could see that he wanted to agree with me.

He wanted to.

But his hands betrayed him. He stretched his fingers and then clenched them into fists, again and again. He wanted to fight. That's what his body was telling me.

I breathed in deeply and considered what I wanted to say next. I knew I could not take it back.

Then I exhaled and I said it.

"If you leave here to go back to your house to get a gun," I said. "You can stay there. I won't let you back here. You will be leaving me. Us."

He stared at me, his jaw slack, and his eyes wide. He looked paralyzed. But I didn't take it back. I meant what I said.

I clenched my lips together and waited for his response. I was furious. I almost wanted him to leave – that's how mad I was.

How enraged I was at the thought that he would endanger Beej or me. Or the beavers.

And then my wish came true.

He bowed his head, briefly, and his gaze went over to Beej, still sleeping. Then he grabbed his hat hanging on a whittled wooden hook by the door, put it on his head, and left.

At first, I felt nothing. A kind of shock, maybe. Numbness. Absence of feeling.

In the vacuum, my mind rushed in.

"You never could trust him anyway," my mind said to me. "Think of how you came across him again in the first place. He had laid a leg trap for one of the beavers! Did he ever even apologize for that? He was showing you who he was. He hasn't changed. Today just confirmed that."

I listened to her ranting for a while, and my body joined in. Grief clenched my chest. An adrenaline lightning came back to my limbs as it had on that night when I ran into the forest and fell. And on that other day.

I started pacing the four steps from one end of the cabin to the other, trying to discharge the energy. Angry. Angry. On fire.

What else could I do now, though? Now that I had this baby. What choices are there for mothers of infants to freak out, to let loose the storms within them, to express the tremendous pressure that builds up when the caretaking of a helpless, dependent being falls upon her? And in a world that has fallen apart?

I decided to swim. Beej was still sleeping, and by the tilt of the sun, I had about a half hour before she woke for an early lunchtime feeding.

The water was colder than it had been the last time I went in – on the evening before Beej was born. I shivered and rubbed my hands against my arms as my legs gradually numbed and accustomed themselves to the temperature. And then I dove in.

My arms stretched long and strong with each stroke as I made my way from one end to the other, taking laps and only pausing for a moment at the end closest to the cabin so I could listen out for the baby's cries. And then I kept going.

I would keep going. This is what my body was telling me as I breathed in the cold November air and then turned my head straight again and felt the warmth of the water passing my face as I exhaled under water in rhythm with the strokes of my arms and kicks of my legs.

"I'm strong," my body said to me. "I can keep going. This will not break you. You have been through worse than this before. I will stay with you. I am your constant companion. Here with you from the beginning. And until the end. I will never leave you. Together, we can raise that child. You can trust me not to hurt you. And the beavers. They will not hurt us. We will not hurt them. This is the wisdom of the animal body that the human mind has forgotten."

Her voice was so clear and sure. It reminded me of my mother's voice when she would comfort me. But there was a difference in it. She was not mothering me. She was an equal to me. We were equal partners, my body and me. And together, we were survivors.

I swam and swam, kicked and floated, on my belly, on my back, even on my sides the way Oma did when we visited her in Germany, and she took us to her community heated indoor pool. As my body moved and spoke to me, my mind grew calmer. I remembered this feeling from long hikes with my mom and Katrina and Mouse.

And from somewhere deep within the recesses of my mind, up floated the German word for hike that Kat had taught me: "Wanderung."

Wandering.

Was that what they were trying to teach me when they brought me here as a child?

How to wander. How to keep going. Wonder. Not knowing. But being. In nature.

These were not sentences, not fully formed thoughts I was having. But there was a kind of correspondence in them between what I was thinking in my mind and what I was feeling in my body.

It felt, dare I say it, good.

Enjoyable. Joyful.

Here I was, swimming back and forth in a chilly beaver pond in the middle of nowhere, and yet it wasn't nowhere. Out there had been nowhere, I saw that now. The world as it had been had removed itself from the world so much that it disappeared. You can't have a world without a world. You can't have wonder without wandering.

My ears perked up when I heard Beej. It was not a cry exactly, but the gentle cooing she sometimes did when first waking. I thought of it as the talking she did to herself as she gradually remembered she was alive.

"Oh, hello eyes blinking. Hello, light. Hello feet kicking. Here I am. Here I am."

I rose from the water, shaking myself to dry off as I'd so often seen the beavers do, and walked quickly to the cabin to catch her before she said hello to her hungry belly and started crying in earnest.

"Hello, Beej. Hi there, baby," I cooed softly as I picked her up. I wrapped my arms around her body and hoped my skin was not too cold and damp from the water.

I settled gently in the middle of the pile of blankets and chose two to wrap around me, creating a little cocoon for her as I offered her my breast.

The let-down of my milk came as a warm feeling rushed through my body and relaxed me. I took a deep breath and let it out.

What had I determined, exactly? What did I know?

Nothing.

I had abandoned any thought of planning or thinking ahead aside from what was right in front of me then: my baby at my breast, my need for my own lunch later, and the gathering of more wood for that night's fire to make dinner and keep me full through the night.

My old self would have seen this as a kind of failure. Certainly, my mind poked up her little head from time to time to question me.

"But what about…? What will you do if…? And how will you…?"

"Hush," I said to my mind. "Just because I don't know the answers to those worries doesn't mean I can't be happy right now, right here, just as I am."

I looked down at Beej as she turned her head up to look at me. This meant that breast was empty, and it was time for me to turn her to the other side.

Even this simple motion she could not manage on her own without me.

But there was no need for worry. Because I was right there. Of that certainty I was completely clear-eyed.

Chap

After the terror of listening to Grayson's encounter with the humans that morning, I could not sleep and spent the day watching the sun throw light and shadows on the sloped walls of our beloved lodge while my family slept beside me.

At one point, I heard something entering the pond, and sniffed until I determined that it was Livia, swimming back and forth. This was good, I thought, that she felt safe enough to come out of the cabin after what had happened.

At sunset, I finally emerged, bleary eyed and jangled, to check on the safety of the pond.

I made my way through the water, sketching a V behind me as I swam, and sniffed and listened.

No humans since that morning. Except the ones we called our friends.

And one of them was sitting on a log to the west, all the way across the pond from their cabin.

After I completed my perimeter, I returned to him, scrambling up the bank and resting beside the cypress log I'd cut that summer, which was now almost completely dry and ready for shredding for winter bedding.

"What's wrong?" I asked Grayson.

"Livia and I had a fight."

"That's not good."

"It wasn't. She was very angry."

"I know how that can be. What was it about if you don't mind my asking?"

"Guns."

"Guns!" I cried before I could stop myself. And then more calmly, I asked, "What about them?"

"After those jerks were here this morning, I told her I wanted to go back to my old house and bring one of my dad's guns here. For protection."

I stayed very still on the outside. Inside, my heart was pounding.

"But she said she wouldn't allow it. I have to say, it was almost harder for me to hear her telling me what to do than for me to hesitate in bringing the gun here right away."

I cocked my head, not sure what he was saying.

"I mean, my mother would never have spoken to my father like that. The way Livia spoke to me. As if she were in charge. Well, she is. That's the thing."

I was still not really understanding.

"She gave me an ultimatum. She said if I got the gun, I couldn't come back. She said that—"

He hesitated.

"She said that she did not want to ruin what we have – what you have – what we all have here. With violence."

I let myself exhale when I heard that. I nodded. I certainly agreed with that.

"Chap," Grayson continued. "I don't know if I can do it. She's asking me to be defenseless. She's making me go against everything I was raised with. I don't know what my father would think of me."

At this, he put his head in his hands and I heard him crying quietly. I waited.

235

"What do you think?" he finally asked. "What should I do?"

I looked out at the pond. I could hear the yearlings stirring. This would be their last winter with us. They would leave in the spring. That was what I told Grayson.

"I have raised nine litters of kits in this pond with Penny," I began. "If I ever worried, if I had doubts, if I was afraid – well, I didn't show it."

He nodded.

"To have a family, you have to believe."

His eyebrows wrinkled at me. I knew he was not understanding yet what I was saying. He reminded me of myself when I was younger and was just beginning to realize what it would mean to have a family. How I would have to change.

"You cannot let yourself worry about what will happen after they leave. Your job is to take care of them and then let them go. Doubting that this will happen will only slow down your work. And work is why you are here. Work is why we are all here – working for those we love, and for all those who depend upon what we do – even those who will never really know what we have done for them."

I saw his left hand rubbing the skin of his chin. I knew he used a sharp thing every morning by the pond to shave his face clean of fur. His gesture reminded me of Penny when she had been thinking about whether to leave the lodge to defend our territory earlier that day.

"Every living being feels fear," I continued. "It's part of the body. It's what allows us to swim faster – or run, in your case. It is a kind of energy. But we cannot let it rule what we do on a regular basis. I could never begin the process of cutting down another tree if I allowed my fear of the tree falling on me to paralyze me."

He pursed his lips and moved his right hand through his hair.

"You're saying a gun is like a tree?" he asked.

"A falling tree," I said. "It's bound to come down to the ground."

"That's what Livia was trying to tell me?"

"I think so," I nodded. "I think what she meant is that she doesn't want you to risk placing Beej and her under that falling tree. If she can help it."

He looked away from me and back out across the pond at their cabin. It was fully dark now, and we watched from the western side of the pond as a gorgeous full moon rose in the east above the water and grazed long fingers of light on the slight ripples there.

We continued pondering about trees and falling and guns and families and our roles in the cycles of all of this as the moon rose before us.

"Did you know that's a beaver moon?" he asked me after this long period of silence. By now the moon was directly overhead.

"What do you mean?" I asked.

"This month's moon. It used to be called a beaver moon because this is the month when you all get busy preparing for the winter."

This struck me. That humans knew this about us and created a name for one of the cycles of the moon to honor us.

"I did not know that," I told him. "But, you know, it isn't just under this moon that we are busy."

"Oh, I know that now for sure," he smiled at me. He was a good man. I was pleased to be his friend.

And I smiled back.

"Well, I guess I'll leave you to your work," he said, standing. He raised his arms above him toward the moon, stretching.

"Have you made your decision?" I asked him.

237

"I have," he said. And he headed back to the cabin.

Livia

I was stoking the fire down by the pond later that afternoon, hoping to hold off the chill as the sun settled into her sleeping place. I had caught two fish and prepared them with a sprinkling of salt and some rosemary Grayson had found growing wild along a roadside outside the swamp where a house and garden probably used to be.

As I placed the deboned fish into the cast iron pan that Grayson had also brought here, it struck me how easily I'd adapted after only a few months. Skinning and deboning fish were easy to me now, as was fishing itself, and starting a fire, and being there.

If I'd been honest with myself, I would have admitted that I'd caught two fish because I was secretly wishing that Grayson would come back. For dinner. Before the dark descended.

He'd been away all day. He'd been gone that long before, but he'd never left without telling me where he was going. To gather mushrooms. To get another few blankets from his old house. To scavenge at an abandoned junk yard for things that we could use around the cabin. He found a wheelbarrow one time. I had no idea how useful that would be until he found the pallets we used to build our cabin.

Always before, he gave me his itinerary so I could picture where he was and estimate how long it would be before he returned. That way, I wouldn't allow myself to worry until he was late.
He'd never been late.

And technically, I supposed he wasn't late now because he didn't tell me he'd be back.

So when the fish was crispy, I flipped them onto an actual plate and started eating with a real fork – which, of course, Grayson had also brought here for us.

Us. Me and Beej? Or the three of us?

I didn't know.

I couldn't know.

Because it wasn't up to me only.

That was the whole point of being in a relationship. You weren't in it alone.

Only the smallest remnants of peach light, glowing like the bottom of a glass jar emptied of the bourbon peach jam that Katrina used to make, were left in the west above the pond when I saw him.

"Go ahead, Liv," I heard Katrina say to me in my memory. "The only way to get it out satisfactorily is with your fingers. A spoon won't do. Not even a knife. I should know," she smiled. "I've tried. Sometimes the only way to get what you want is to use your own hands."

Her voice receded in my head as Grayson came closer. Slowly. Sometimes looking at me, sidelong glances, before his head tipped down to the ground again. He was getting closer. But he wasn't sure of himself. I knew him well enough to know this just from looking at how he was walking.

I knew him.

That thought struck me. I put down the plate. I stood up.

There were a million things I didn't know. If the world as we knew it would ever come back. If the grief I still felt swimming in my chest after all the deaths would ever go away. How long I could survive like this. What would happen to Beej as she grew older. Whether I could protect her.

But I knew him.

That was one thing I knew for certain, as he made his way closer to me around the circle of the pond.

So I went to him.

"Use your hands," Kat whispered to me.

When I got close enough, I opened my arms and spread my fingers wide. I did not open my mouth. There was nothing I could say that would express my relief and also my grief at what we'd been through. Separately before we knew each other. Together once we did.

And now? I did not know. But I knew that I knew him. And that was all I needed to know.

He hesitated. He looked at me, briefly, then looked down again. He had come back, at least this far. But he wasn't sure, now that he was here, if he could come back all the way. That's what he was saying in that pause.

I waited.

I did not move. I did not go closer. I did not force myself on him or insist that he hurry in his decision.

I waited.

He walked past me.

Chap

"Papa, what is happening?" Gigi asked me as we paused our work on the poplar trees under the light of the full moon.

I looked up to see what she was seeing. The moon was disappearing.

"It's kind of scary," she said.

Henry and Mack stopped trimming the branches along the path we were creating so the larger poplar logs could be taken to the pond and joined us as they heard us talking.

"I heard mama talking about this once!" Mack said, his voiced filled with excitement.

"What is it?" Henry asked, more serious.

"There is nothing to be afraid of," I reassured them. "This is something that happens from time to time. I've seen it several times before in my life. What happens is that sometimes the earth is lined up between the sun and the moon just right, and the sun's light that usually lights the moon is blocked by the roundness of the earth and we see all the shapes of the moon in one night."

Henry thought about this and said, "So it's kind of like time speeding up."

"Maybe," I said. "You could look at it like that. But really, it's also an opportunity to slow down and see what is always already happening."

"Like with the kits," Gigi said. "I feel like when I play with them lately, time is passing more quickly, but also, I appreciate each tiny moment so much. Every little thing they do. It's so cute to watch them growing and discovering."

I nodded. "Yes, Gigi. It is exactly like that."

Then Mack chimed in, but his tone was different. "I felt like this in the trap," he said softly. "I thought about my life. I felt the moments stretching out before me. I did not know what would happen to me next. But I saw everything that I had had up to that time in a new way. Brighter. You. My family. This pond. Our home. The trees. The water. Even the hickories standing there watching me, with their long leaves like many paws hanging down as if they would help me if they could. I saw everything so vividly."

I placed my paw on his back and nuzzled closer to him. Gigi did the same on the other side.

"We are so glad you came back to us," she said.

"Yes, we are," Henry agreed. "We were all so worried about you."

I knew this would be one of the last full moons I would have with the three of them, and it certainly would most likely be the only time we would witness an eclipse together, so I suggested that we go get their mother and brothers and sisters to join us.

As we passed by the cabin on the way back to the pond, we saw Grayson and Livia and Beej sitting by their fire. They were also watching the moon.

"Henry," I said. "Go across to the other side of the pond to ask your mother and the kits to join us."

He did, and Mack and Gigi and I waited in the water, floating on our backs in the shallow area and munching on some roots. The moon was fully in the west now, and I decided that this side of the pond was best for viewing, but I didn't want to disturb Livia and Grayson, who seemed fully engaged in something just then.

Before too long, I heard the splashing and laughing of the six little ones as they made their way toward us across the water. Happy and Hero arrived first, as they almost always did, trying to emulate their big brother, Henry, who had taken it upon himself to teach them to be responsible and strong in the same ways that he was.

Next were Gaia and Gem, who sailed up to Gigi and circled around her, giggling. The three of them were almost always laughing and joking together, and already I could feel how much the little ones would miss Gigi when she left in the spring. We all still had a winter together, though, I reminded myself. No reason to mourn what had not yet happened and ruin the time we did still have.

The slowest ones were Mick and Meadow, who stayed close to Penny as she swam behind them all to protect them from any predators who might be following. The two of them had become a bit hesitant and clung closer to their mother since the day that Mack had been away from us for so long. I hoped their next two years with us would bolster their courage and allow them to build greater trust in themselves.

Penny nuzzled against me in the water and said, "It's been a while since we had so many kits to watch the moon like this, hasn't it?"

"It certainly has," I said, nuzzling her in return and purring softly. My love for her had only grown over the years, and deep within me like the water tables that we helped to fill rose such great gratitude and love for her and all the years we'd been together in this life.

I looked around at all of us, eleven happy, healthy beavers, floating and enjoying the night under this beaver moon, the name that Grayson had taught me for this month when we do the last of our preparations to fill the cache and strengthen the lodge before the first of winter's chill.

Livia

All at once I was furious again.

"Where are you going?" I yelled after him as he continued to walk away. "What are you doing? Why did you come back?"

He stopped briefly, and I could sense the muscles in his back clenching against the pummeling of my voice.

Where did this anger in me come from? I'd never been this mad at anyone before. Not even when they'd left me. For real. By dying.

Here he was, about twenty feet in front of me, and the fact that he had not come to my open arms, accepted my invitation for a reunion, and walked away from me, and would not look at me now – it ignited a rage in me.

"Talk to me!" I yelled.

He turned around. There were tears in his eyes. He raised his hand to wipe them away, and then he took off his hat and threw it to the ground.

"I don't want to talk to you!" he snarled.

"Why?" I asked, almost screaming. And then my tears started. I sat down on the ground, sobbing.

"Why?" I asked again, more softly.

He came back and sat down next to me.

For a long time he didn't talk. He didn't look at me. He didn't offer me his hand. We just sat crying together.

It reminded me of our first night together.

"You can't tell me what to do," he said, finally. Softly.

I started to argue. I thought of my rage and desire to protect Beej. And then I heard Kat within me again.

"No words," she said. "Touch."

So I reached out my hand.

He took it.

"You can't tell me what to do," he said again. "Just as I can't tell you what to do. But I heard you. I would rather be here with you without a gun than anywhere else in the world with one."

I smiled through my tears.

"Thank you," I whispered.

And just then, at that moment, those were words enough.

But later that night, as Grayson and I sat by the firepit we'd built together with a circle of stones and watched the beaver moon rising as Beej slept soundly in her cradle nearby, I felt more words, deeper words, rising from within me.

I decided to tell him the story.

He already knew the story of my family and how Mouse and I became best friends and sisters, and how our moms were best friends before they became lovers and got married. He knew the origins of Beej's story, too— and I had even told him what I did after that.

"Nothing to be ashamed of, Liv," he'd said to me then. "Nothing at all."

And, of course, he knew the story of how Chap had helped me on that full moon night that Beej came into the world. How I learned to listen to him and understand what he was saying. And that once I did this, I could talk with all of them. They'd become my friends and family, just like Mouse and Katrina had become my family.

He knew all these stories about me and he accepted them. He accepted me.

Over time, he had even learned the language of the beavers, too – and he told me about the conversation he'd had with Chap that very evening.

But there was another story that had not been told. And in the exhilaration and exhaustion created by our reunion, as we sat warm and safe by the fire and the moon glowed above us, I decided it was time.

"I need to tell you something," I began.

"Okay," he said, and I could see the light of the fire dancing in his brown eyes as he nodded.

"It's what was underneath my reaction when you suggested getting a gun."

He turned to look at me.

"My dad was not a good person," I said and then stopped. This was harder than I thought it would be.

"I was a baby, and then a toddler, when he and my mom were together. So I don't have many clear memories. No, that's not really right. The memories I have are very clear."

I looked up at the moon and noticed a pinkish glow around it. I thought of myself as a baby. I imagined my mother holding me in a soft pink blanket. My heart clenched at the understanding I now had, as a mother myself, for what she must have felt.

"It's just that they're not really stories," I continued telling him. "They're feelings that live in me. Even now. All this time later. A stomachache. My heartbeat racing. Feeling like I can't breathe."

He reached over and took my hand but said nothing. He waited for me to keep going.

"He beat her." There. I had said it. "He pulled her hair and he pushed her. He kicked her on the kitchen floor. She tried to hide under the table. He screamed at her and said awful things. I hear them now, in my head. I saw this. I saw it from there on the floor. I hid under the kitchen table with her. But he knew I was there. She knew, too. She knew what I was seeing."

There was anger in my voice, but saying these words out loud, something else was covering the anger like the pink light starting to cover the moon.

"I was so mad at my mother," I said, finally, after all this time, crying with the grief I'd been burying.

"I hated her. I hated him for what he did, but in my little girl way, there was a deeper feeling of rage toward her. I hated how weak she was. How she cowered and hid her face when he beat her. Went down on the floor, legs and arms tucked under her, knowing I was there. Watching. I wanted her to fight back. I wanted her to take me away. I blamed her," I said, finally catching my breath.

"That's the truth. I blamed her and I never really forgave her. Until the last day of her life."

He stroked my hand in both of his but stayed quiet, listening to the shuddering in my body as the tears receded.

I continued in a whisper. Slowly. "Grayson, I cannot take the chance that I would allow myself to become like her. I cannot do that to my daughter. I will not live with violence. Of any kind. That's why I was so adamant about the gun. I cannot allow it. I can't."

He nodded and said, "I would never."

I tried to smile, but only a corner of my mouth curled up. "I know you think that. But accidents happen. We don't even have a way to lock the gun away out here. I do not want to take even the slightest chance that Beej would witness violence."

He took a deep breath and sighed. "I hear you, Livia. I'm sorry for what happened to you. And your mom. I will never do that to you. I promise. With all my heart."

"I know it," I said. "I just wanted to explain it to you. It wasn't right for me to get so angry at you. And I'm sorry. I wanted to explain."

"Thank you," he said. And then he leaned down to pick up Beej, who was starting to fuss for her late-night snack, and as he placed her gently into my arms, he kissed me.

The moon was disappearing. It was like a full cycle of moon in one night. After the pink ring around it turned to a reddish glow, we could see the moon begin to wane.

"An eclipse!" I whispered in awe. "My mom loved stuff like this. She set us up in the yard at night so we could watch on lawn chairs with hot chocolate and piles of blankets over us."

"My dad loved them, too," he said. "My mom was more skeptical. She had weird ideas about nature left over from the church she went to as a kid. So she never came out to see it like we did. And when I was old enough, my dad would plan camping trips for us so we could see it far from any lights."

We sat quietly thinking of our parents as Beej nursed and then fell asleep again. Even my dad was on my mind in a way I hadn't allowed him to be in a very long time. That was when it struck me. Beej already shared my legacy. She, too, came from a history of violence.

Maybe there was nothing I could do to prevent it, after all.

Or maybe she could one day live up to her name and be the beginning of something new. Something better. For people and the beavers both. Beaver Girl. I might not live to see it, but I could do my best to try to make it possible.

"Grayson?" I asked quietly. "Can I ask you something?"

"Sure," he said. "Anything."

"Will you marry me?"

His grin just about lit up the pond in front of us under the dark of the moon.

"Why, of course! I'd be honored!" he answered.

I leaned over to hand the sleeping baby to him and then I stood up. I knew what I was looking for. I felt around in the dark to the left side of our cabin where a large willow had begun dropping its leaves to prepare for the winter. When willow leaves were green, they were long and supple and provided shade on hot days, but when they dropped, they became brown and curled up like rings. I found some and held them in my hands to head back to Grayson.

Once next to the light of the fire pit again, I opened my palm and picked the best one before laying the rest of them down on the ground.

I held it out to him and smiled. "This is me, asking for your hand in marriage, right now. Will you stay with me and be my husband? Will you raise Beej with me as your daughter? Will you promise to love us and be good to us, all the rest of your life?"

There were tears in his eyes as he smiled at me and said, "I most surely do."

I put the curled leaf on the ring finger of his left hand.

Then he reached down to the ground to sift through the other leaves and picked one.

"Livia, will you do me the honor of being my wife, my best friend, my partner for life? I promise to be good to you and Beej and never hurt you, never leave you, and take care of you and our home and everyone who lives here, too, as best I can. Will you do me the honor of this?"

I laughed from joy and said, "Oh, yes, of course I do!"

We kissed as the moon was growing big again, and the light was expanding within me, too. I felt it from my toes to my belly and up to my heart and all the way into my head, a bubbling, blissful feeling. I was now a newly and happily married woman with my best friend at my side and our daughter cradled between us. We were the parents of beaver girl under the growing light of beaver moon.

Chap

I gazed over toward the humans who, I knew from talking with Grayson earlier, had healing to do to stay together at the pond permanently.

He waved to me.

"Chap," he called. "Come on over. All y'all. We have some news to tell you."

Penny whistled to the kits to gather more closely together, and we all scrambled up the bank, the littlest ones slipping slightly as they gained their footing on the muddy surface.

What a curious sight we all were under the increasingly bright light of the beaver moon! I shook my head in wonder, knowing how precious this all was – not just the moon and the many kits and the humans who had become our friends and family – but all of it. Life itself and the turning of time and tides and moon and light and shadow and the way, as we'd been discussing right before this, that there are moments when we appreciate it all for the deep beauty and abiding love that exists in everything.

We arranged ourselves around the fire, Penny admonishing the little ones not to get too close, and I could see the delight in their eyes, perhaps caused more by this rare opportunity for them to be safely near fire than from the moon's eclipse, which they were too young to appreciate fully.

Meadow snuggled next to Livia's leg, and I saw Livia gesture to Grayson to take the baby so she could pick up Meadow and put her onto her lap.

"Penny, Chap," Grayson said. "And Henry, Hero, Happy, Mack, Mick, Meadow, and Gigi, Gaia and Gem." With each name he looked at each one of us and smiled at us. "We have some good news. We got married tonight."

I saw the kits' eyes squinch with questions.

"That means they have promised to be partners for life," I explained to them.

"Well, congratulations!" chimed Penny. "We are very happy for you! And we hope that you will always be happy here!"

"I guess I'm confused," said Gigi. "I already thought you were partners."

"Well," said Livia. "Yes. That's true. But we made it official." She showed us her finger with a willow leaf wrapped around it. Grayson had one, too.

What weird creatures these humans are! I thought. That they would need a leaf on their hands to make something real.

"I hope my kits find partners as good to each other as I know you two are," I said.

And I meant it.

This was something we did share with the humans – a desire for partnership and equality and a belief in the importance of family and hard work that we each did separately for the good of the whole.

"Thank you," said Livia, and Gaia and Gem crawled onto her lap as soon as Meadow scrambled down. She held her arms around them as if they were her own.

"Can I touch the baby?" asked Mick.

"Certainly," said Grayson after Livia nodded and smiled. Mick moved slowly and carefully and then patted the skin of her little chubby cheek.

"She's so warm even though she has no fur!" he exclaimed, pulling his paw back, and everyone laughed.

"That's true," said Livia. "We are not as lucky as you. We need clothes and blankets and fire to keep us warm when it gets colder. You have this nice, warm fur."

The moon was almost round again, and its dazzling light was reflected in the roundness of the pond. It felt even more bright after the recent darkness.

"I have something else to say," said Grayson, and I knew he was talking to us, the beavers, and that Livia was not sure what was coming next. I saw her eyebrows wrinkle to each other as she listened.

"The promise I made to Livia tonight," he began. "That was not just for her alone. It was also for Beej, of course, as I am her father now and vow to raise her with love and steadiness."

He looked around at all of us.

"I also included all of you in this promise. I have learned so many things from Liv," he said, and nodded his head at her. "But I've also learned so much from all of you. I am not the same person I was on that day."

He stopped and looked directly at Mack.

"Mack," he said. "I am sorry for what I did to you. I was different then. I was hungry. I was not raised to know that beavers were so smart and such hard workers and so caring towards the earth and the water and their families. I did not know all this before."

He handed the baby back to Livia as the kits scampered down from her lap, and he put his hands on his heart.

"Mack, please forgive me," he said.

Mack closed his eyes and bowed his head. I knew he was remembering that day in deeper ways than any of us would ever know. Then he lifted his head and looked directly at Grayson as he said, "I forgive you."

"Thank you," Grayson sighed, and then continued. "What I want you all to know is that when I married Livia tonight, I also married all of y'all."

Gaia and Gem giggled.

"What I mean is that I will do all I can here at the beaver pond, which was your home originally, to care for it and to keep it safe. And to keep it peaceful."

I saw Livia smiling with a look on her face that I had never seen from her before. As if she had long ago stepped on a burr that lodged in her paw, and after being there and causing her pain for a very long time, it had finally made its way out.

"Thank you," she said to Grayson. And she leaned over to kiss him. Gem and Gaia giggled again.

Even though the moon was still bright in the west, I noticed the first light of dawn just beginning to glow on the eastern horizon at the same time as Penny said, "Well, it's time for all these kits to head to bed."

Livia nodded and sighed. "We haven't slept at all, either. I guess we've been keeping beaver hours tonight."

We all laughed.

Each of the eleven kits said goodbye to all three of them, as Grayson and Livia patted their backs softly and wished them a good sleep.

In turn, each beaver kit patted Beej with their little paws softly on her hands and shoulders and arms.

Penny said once more to them, "Thank you for sharing your good news with us. I am very glad that we are all a family." And then she swam back to the lodge with the kits.

I stayed behind because I had one more thing that I wanted to say even though the sunlight was growing gold and bright behind the trees.

"Thank you for all you've both done to understand us."

Tears welled in Livia's eyes.

"I love you, Chap," she said.

Grayson nodded slowly, smiling. "I love you, too," he said to me.

"And I love you, too," I said. And then I headed to my lodge to settle into my crowded but warm and cozy bed, safe and sound and surrounded by my growing, happy, human and beaver family.

END

Cassie Premo Steele, Ph.D., is a lesbian, ecofeminist poet and novelist, whose writing focuses on the themes of trauma and the environment. She has published many books, including most recently the poetry book, *Swimming in Gilead,* and the novel, *Beaver Girl.* Her writing has won many awards, including the Archibald Rutledge Prize named after the first Poet Laureate of South Carolina, where she lives with her wife. www.cassiepremosteele.com